Escape from the Mansion
on the Island of Doctor Grimdeath

Escape from the Mansion on the Island of Doctor Grimdeath

Doug Bedwell

Space Bear Press
Cloverdale, Indiana

This book is a work of fiction. The characters, incidents, and dialogue are drawn from the author's imagination. No direct reference to any specific events, organizations, monsters, college students or professors, or any other sorts of persons is intended.

And *please*, no spoilers!

For information, please contact:
  Space Bear Press
  P.O. Box 182
  Cloverdale, IN   46120

  On the web at: spacebearpress.com
  Our online store: https://space-bear-press.square.site/
  On Facebook at: Facebook.com/spacebearpress

Bedwell, Doug
        [Suspense; Horror; Comedy]
        Escape from the Mansion on the Island of Doctor Grimdeath
        First Edition: August 1, 2020
        ISBN-13: 978-1-943219-13-1 (Paperback)
        ISBN-13: 978-1-943219-14-8 (Hardcover)

Original Cover Artwork © Amy Nagi – www.amynagi.com
Cover and Interior Layout and Design by Doug Bedwell

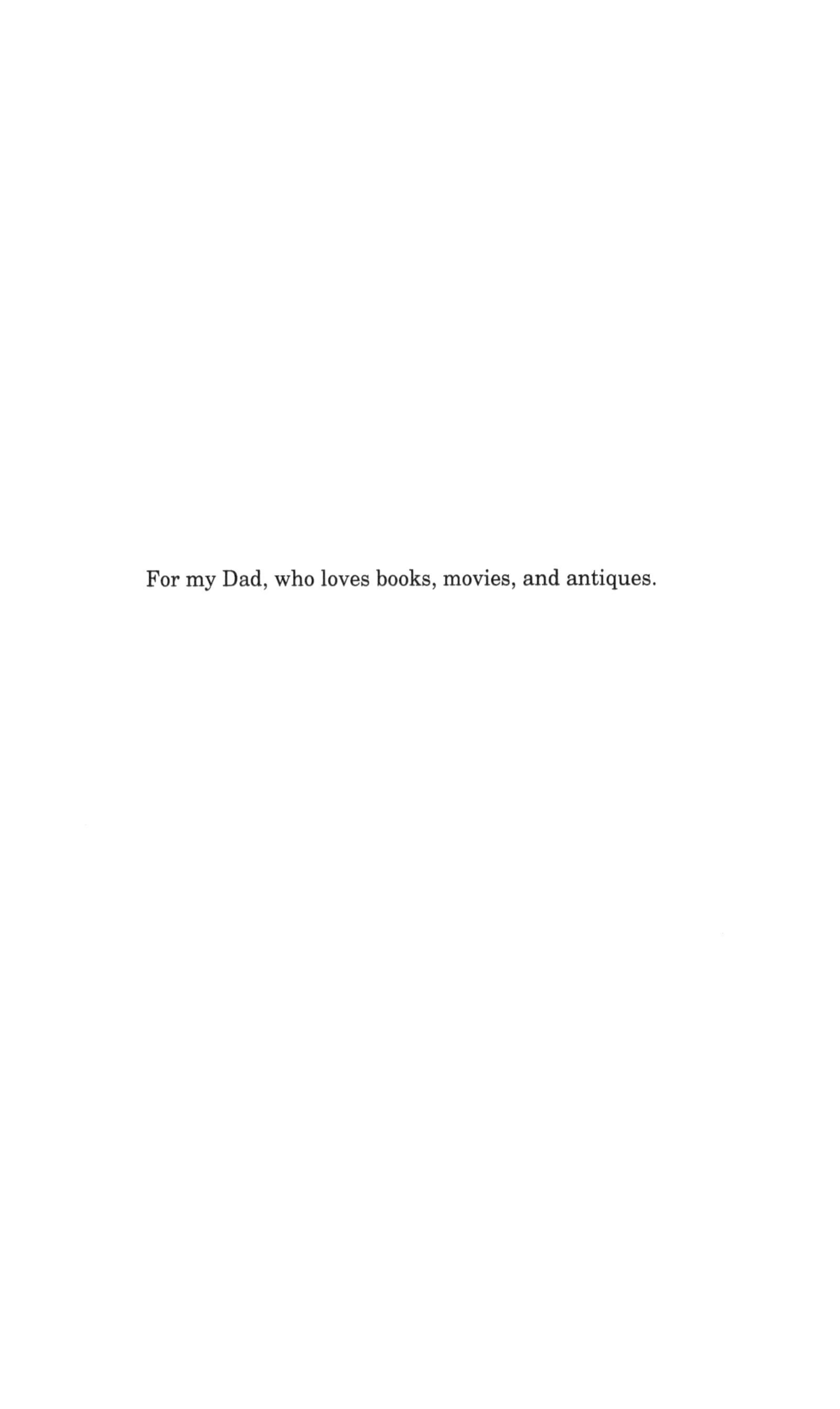

For my Dad, who loves books, movies, and antiques.

Chapter One:
The Arrival

The sun – predictably enough – was setting. On the far horizon, ominous clouds were gathering, and the evening breeze was swirling in all directions. It seemed that, more than likely, this would be a dark and stormy night.

Shelby Oswald's long blonde hair was billowing with the wind as she stood at the forward rail of the charter boat and gazed across the choppy water, watching the little island draw ever closer. The island, as well as the darkly brooding mansion which loomed upon the low hill at its center, was the property of the fabulously wealthy and eccentric Professor Grimdeath, or "Doctor G" as he was more commonly referred to (with varying degrees of awe, suspicion, and fear) on the Dume University campus. Tonight, the eight students from his seminar course *Horror in Popular Culture and Practice* would be arriving at this foreboding and isolated locale, ostensibly for the administration of their final exam.

Shelby, of course, was one of those students. Like so many others, she had signed up for the seminar without any clear idea of what exactly it would entail; the professor's reputation alone had been enticement enough. However, though at first the class roster was quite large – with over a hundred students registered across four separate sections – their numbers had steadily dwindled over the course of the semester, as students either dropped out or transferred into less difficult courses. Doctor G was a demanding and unforgiving instructor, best kept at arm's length by those hoping to keep their grade point averages intact. And yet, for some few intrepid students like Shelby, the heightened challenge only added to the appeal.

The first few class sessions had covered a dizzying array of literature and film, referencing well-worn classics such as *Frankenstein* and *Dracula*, but also delving into subjects that ranged from medieval alchemy to black magic, before broadening the scope of inquiry to more esoteric topics such as voodoo, Egyptian embalming, Mayan blood rituals, and (eventually) reality television. Later course sessions had involved focused lab work in such diverse fields as cinematography, cloning, robotics, botany, audio engineering, artificial intelligence, and contemporary fashion design.

Shelby had eagerly devoured it all, even to the point of neglecting assignments from her other courses. She had become enraptured with a newfound enthusiasm for the sinister, mysterious, and bizarre. It might fairly be said that the semester had left her a little unhinged, though arguably in a largely benign and down-to-earth way. But whatever her initial motives in signing up for the course might have been, her ultimate goal was now within sight. If only she could pass this final exam, she would have made it through the toughest course, taught by the toughest instructor that Dume University had to offer, and all the other members of the school's cheerleading squad could shove it.

Unfortunately, however, Shelby would very likely not be completing her final examination. In fact, she would soon be facing a particularly bloody and untimely end, in about eighty-five pages, somewhere near the end of Chapter Nineteen. Had she been aware of this fact, Shelby might not have been quite so eager to visit the island at all. But then again, perhaps she still would have. If the truth be told, over the course of the past semester Shelby had become so enamored with the myriad mysteries of the arcane, that even the prospect of death (or some other unthinkable fate) might well not have deterred her from risking just one more peek behind the infinite curtain.

And – as we have paused for the moment to contemplate Shelby Oswald's potentially abbreviated destiny – it may be worth noting that she would likely have found a certain measure of consolation in the fact that, among her classmates, she would not be the first to go.

"SCARED?" shouted Carson McBride, who had quietly crept up behind her. Shelby's heart skipped a beat, and she clutched the rail a little more tightly, before turning her head just far enough to look back at him over her shoulder.

"Exciting stuff!" Carson continued, apparently pleased with himself that he'd succeeded at startling her. "Just like the movies," he added, before making a purely gratuitous thumbs-up gesture with both hands, and flashing Shelby a winning smile.

Carson was tall, dark-haired and good looking. A senior Theatre major with a minor in Business Marketing, he'd been voted *Most Likely to be Cast as the Romantic Lead in a Life Insurance Commercial* four years running. Most of his peers assumed that after graduation he would abandon the arts entirely, eventually settling into a comfortably anonymous career selling used cars, or women's shoes, or dental implants, or low-grade wicker lawn furniture.

But Carson had greater ambitions than that, and much more elaborate plans for his future – plans which he hoped Doctor Grimdeath's seminar would help make possible. And now, with the long semester behind him, all that remained was to ace the final exam.

He never doubted that everything would work out splendidly, at least for himself. He had, to this point in his relatively brief existence on planet Earth, breezed through life with the sort of benighted calm and unshakeable self-confidence that only the beautiful people can ever attain. The possibility of failure never daunted nor even occurred to him. Deep in his heart he knew without question that, regardless of any obstacle, his personal charm would always carry the day.

Shelby had taken an immediate dislike to him.

In the cockpit of the charter yacht, the boat pilot stood at the wheel, whistling breezily to himself in a wavering and uncertain tune. He was a plump and weatherbeaten old soul, with calloused hands, a wrinkled face, and an unshaven whiskery scruff of a white beard. Thinning tufts of unkempt hair poked out from under his well-worn brown and orange baseball cap.

Nearby, Rodney Halifax and Shondra James stood at the boat's starboard railing, looking out toward the gathering stormclouds that were slowly overtaking the rosy glow of the sunset. The whole of the angry sky was reflected in the rippling waves that rolled past the swiftly moving ship.

Rodney took a quick sip from his water bottle and checked his watch. The watch said that it was 7:39 PM. The water bottle said that it was not filled with water, but rather with a carefully blended concoction which Rodney found a little more bracing. Rodney shivered with the chill of the wind, gazed down the length of the boat toward the fast-approaching island, and decided that a little more bracing was definitely called for. He took another sip, and winced. It was, he thought to himself darkly, going to be one of those nights.

Rodney had always had a somewhat nervous disposition, and a semester with Doctor Grimdeath had done him no favors in that regard. Thinking back on it now, he realized that he should have dropped the course during the first week of classes, or better yet never signed up for it at all. And yet, for reasons that were not entirely clear even to himself, he'd toughed it out to the end. Now if he could only nurse his tattered nerves along for one more night, he'd finally be able to relax and recover. But he knew full well that wasn't going to be easy; and even the boatman's eerie little tune was already setting him on edge.

"I'm sorry, would you mind not whistling?" Rodney said as politely as he could. "It gives me the willies."

"What is that, anyway?" Shondra asked. "It sounds familiar, but I can't place it."

"It's a catchy little number, isn't it?" the pilot replied, in his low-pitched and gravelly voice. He made an odd clicking sound with his tongue, then returned to his whistling as before.

A few seconds later, without warning, the pilot suddenly veered the boat sharply to port, narrowly avoiding one of the many hidden reefs of jagged rocks that surrounded the Doctor's private island. A moment later he corrected the ship's course just as violently back to starboard, aiming the prow once again toward the little sheltered cove and sandy stretch of beach, where a long wooden pier jutted out some fifty feet into the shallow water.

Rodney clutched at the ship's railing and frowned. He'd come to the conclusion that talking with the boat pilot was a bad idea while steering through dangerous waters, and he more than half-suspected that the resulting conversation wouldn't be worth the trouble anyway. He looked out at the rippling waves, and gave some serious thought to throwing up.

But even as Rodney turned his attention to more pressing concerns, Shondra James was still contemplating the boat pilot and his curious whistling. Shondra was a fifth-year senior, finishing up some general distribution courses in her final semester. She would soon be graduating, or so she hoped, as a double major in Sports Medicine and Music Theory. She had an excellent ear for melody and, listening to the pilot's whistling, it seemed to her that the tune sounded a bit like the opening movement of Mendelssohn's Violin Concerto in E Minor.

Only played backwards.

On a theremin.

Chapter 2:
The Head Count

As the boat pulled smoothly into the sheltered little cove, there was no one waiting at the dock to greet them, and no other watercraft were anywhere to be seen. In fact had the students not known better, they might have thought the place was entirely deserted, or more accurately, *abandoned*. Aside from the ponderous and weatherworn pier, the only structure they could see was a tumble-down little woodframe shack with unpainted clapboard siding, which appeared to be either an old boathouse or some sort of disused tool shed. Though the mansion itself had been clearly visible as the yacht first approached, from their current vantage point it was hidden from view by the low trees and the heavy brush that covered most of the island.

Before being allowed to debark, the students were gathered together on the yacht's foredeck by a hunched and severe looking young man dressed in a dark shirt and tie. He had a crooked shoulder, thin brown hair, and a penetrating gaze made all the more disconcerting by the fact that his right eye seemed to be somewhat larger than his left. In his right hand he held a large brown clipboard, while his left hand fidgeted absently with a ball point pen.

The young man's name was Gregor Karmazoff, and he'd become a familiar presence to the students over the course of the semester. Only a few years before, he'd been just like them: simply one more nearly anonymous young undergraduate at Dume University. But having lasted eight semesters with Doctor G as his academic advisor, Gregor elected to continue with post-graduate study, and had stayed on as a teaching assistant.

He had been working closely with Professor Grimdeath for nearly five years now, and had changed a great deal in that time. He'd once been tall and athletic, with a sharply inquisitive nature and an easy air of confidence. No more. Now he was thin and drawn, a bent and uneasy figure with nervous hands and an odd twitch in his left cheek that he could not entirely control. The cause of this transformation was easy enough to explain: Gregor Karmazoff had quite simply seen too much.

He had been waiting at the mainland dock as the students first arrived, taking the roll and handing out some last-minute paperwork for each of them to sign. But no one other than the boat pilot had noticed that he'd also come aboard for the trip to the island. Gregor had quietly kept himself locked in a small private cabin, and the other students – if they'd given the matter any thought at all – had naturally assumed that he'd stayed behind on the mainland.

"Welcome..." he said in a dramatically clipped and sinister tone, "to the island of Doctor Grimdeath." He gave the slightest nod of his asymmetrical head, then forced his face into something that resembled a smile. As if on cue, a low roll of thunder rumbled softly, somewhere in the distance.

"Signatures, signatures..." Gregor added, almost cheerfully. "No one goes ashore until I have collected your requisite forms."

The students handed him their completed documents – some more enthusiastically than others – and Gregor carefully checked each one to make sure it had been correctly filled out and signed. The first of the two forms was an ordinary non-disclosure agreement. Though the students had been studying under the good doctor for the entire semester, none of them (excepting Gregor) had been allowed to visit the island before. This was the doctor's private estate and inner sanctum. Here, he carried out his most important research and his most secret experiments. As such, the need for a legally binding non-disclosure agreement was, at minimum, quite understandable.

But the second form was slightly more unnerving, and came as something of a surprise to all of the students. It was a special waiver, indemnifying the good Doctor of any liability whatsoever in the unfortunate event that some form of personal injury might befall a student during the course of the examination. The form was broadly worded to cover almost any eventuality imaginable, including everything from physical disfiguration to psychological distress, to even an irreversible and horrifically gruesome death.

This was the part the professor's assistant had most been looking forward to... collecting those signatures. The students could only imagine what might be in store for them on this night; but Gregor Karmazoff *knew*. This was the key moment. Once they had signed and handed over those documents, the dice – as the saying goes – were cast. There could be no retractions. No one would be able to back out, not that Gregor expected any of them to try. He smiled tautly to himself, licking his lips ever so slightly, as if he were savoring the thought.

"And one final item," Gregor added, once he had all the necessary documents in hand. "If you will please relinquish any electronic devices you may have brought with you. They are not to be allowed."

"Including our phones?" asked Meridian Palmer, with evident alarm. Meridian, or "Meri" as she preferred to be called, was a thin, lanky young woman, fashionably clad in ragged designer jeans, and sporting a trendily angular haircut. Her major was Electrical Engineering, with an emphasis on Digital Technology. Though her classmates certainly knew her by sight – it's hard to go entirely unnoticed in a class of only eight – to that point, few of the other students had ever spoken with her at any length, and one or two of them weren't even certain of her name. She tended to keep to herself, and to keep her nose firmly pressed against her smartphone most of the time, rarely bothering to look up or otherwise engage with anyone.

"No cameras," the professor's assistant repeated, to firmly clarify the matter. "No pictures; No websearches; No help from the studio audience."

"But what if there's an emergency?" Meri insisted. "What if we need to call for help?"

"Then I suggest you scream," Gregor replied, without the slightest hint of a smile. "As loudly as possible."

That ended the debate, such as it was. Each of the students surrendered their various phones and tablets and smart-watches without further complaint, carefully depositing them into a small cardboard box.

"We will get them back, won't we?" asked Shondra, reluctantly.

"After the examination, of course," Gregor replied, "That is... assuming you will *want* them."

"Of course we'll want them back," Meri insisted, testily. "What are you going to do with them?"

"Nothing at all," the professor's assistant replied. "Your phones, at least, will survive the night, untouched and undamaged." Gregor could not help smiling at his own dark little joke, as he neatly checked off the last item from his clipboard itinerary.

"And congratulations to you all," he continued. "The preliminaries are now complete, and you may proceed to the main event. There is a cobblestone footpath at the end of the pier which will take you directly to the mansion. I would suggest that you hurry along there now, as your time is running short. You will receive your final instructions in the grand foyer, just inside the main entrance."

"Aren't you coming with us?" Rodney asked, uneasily.

"No." replied Gregor, without further explanation.

"Will the professor be meeting us inside, then?" Shondra asked.

"The boat will return tomorrow morning," Gregor continued, deliberately ignoring her question. "A pleasant good evening to you all. And farewell."

With that, he turned sharply away, walked briskly back toward the boat's interior, and soon disappeared from view. The students stood in uncomfortable silence for a few moments staring after him, until the old boat pilot cleared his throat loudly, and gestured toward the extended gangplank.

The students took the hint, and one by one they carefully filed ashore. Once all eight of his young passengers had reached the wooden dock, the pilot flipped the switch on his control panel to retract the hydraulic ramp, threw the boat's engines sharply into reverse, and soon the charter yacht was clear of the dock and racing away across the choppy water toward the mainland.

Carson McBride took a few confident strides out to the end of the pier, raised a hand to his forehead and gave a quick salute in the direction of the departing boat.

"Thanks for everything!" he shouted. "You've been a great help! It's been wonderful studying with you!"

Carson planted his hands firmly on his hips and seemed even more pleased with himself than usual, despite the fact that his resonant baritone voice had been drowned out by the roar of the engines and the churning of the water in the vessel's wake. It was unlikely that either Gregor or the boat pilot had heard him, not that his glad-handing would have made the slightest difference to either of them.

"How thrilling!" Carson added cheerfully, before turning back to the group with a self-satisfied nod. "What a great opportunity this whole semester has been, hasn't it? I'm sure looking forward to our final exam, though I hate to see it all come to an end. Ah, the joys of learning! What good clean fun."

As the sun inched its way below the horizon and the island slowly dwindled into the distance behind them, Gregor Karmazoff emerged once again from his private cabin, and climbed the little metal ladder to the ship's upper platform. The boat pilot cast a sideways glance in the teaching assistant's general direction, clicked his tongue several times, and gave a confidential little nod.

"I've got twenty bucks that says the cute blonde makes the grade," he said. He squinted slightly and raised one of his bushy eyebrows, to punctuate the dare.

Gregor was having none of it.

"I've got fifty that says that none of them do," he snorted dismissively. "And the blonde doesn't stand a chance."

"The movie..." the old man countered sagely, "...doesn't always follow the screenplay." He clicked his tongue once more, nodding confidently. "You can think what you like," he added, "but my money's on that little blonde, all the same."

"I'll take that bet," Gregor replied. "And double or nothing that not a single one of them makes it through the night alive."

Chapter 3:
The Island

Doctor Alistair Grimdeath was a true renaissance man: a polymath and master of many fields, both commonplace and obscure. As *Professori Emeritus Ultimatum* at Dume University, he had over his long career taught courses ranging from archaeology to folklore; from chemical engineering to popular culture; from art history to forensic medicine; from artificial intelligence to flower arrangement. He never taught more than a single class each semester, and never repeated any course that he had taught before. Some years, he taught no courses at all.

The university brass quietly tolerated his eccentricities, partly because the arcane rules of academic tenure made it virtually impossible for them to dismiss him, but more importantly because of the enormous prestige, notoriety, and intangible mystique his presence lent to the whole university. For a relatively small, otherwise unheralded institution like Dume, having a man of such formidable international reputation – even if that reputation was a somewhat suspect one – was worth almost any inconvenience. So for the most part, Professor Grimdeath was given free reign to research and teach whatever he felt like, semester to semester. Genius has its privileges.

Though he had been formally granted unlimited access to the equipment and resources of every academic department, he rarely made use of them. For all of his most important research he preferred to sequester himself on his isolated little island, working exclusively at his secure private facilities there, far away from inquisitive university administrators, or any other prying eyes.

And, as far as anyone knew, his work was done entirely at his own expense. He never drew financial resources from the university coffers at all, aside from his modest salary. Nor did he seem to draw funds from any public foundations or research grants. But whether his primary funding came from his own considerable fortune, or from some other secretive undisclosed private source, no one ever pressed him for the details. The accountants at the Dume University budgeting office had long ago concluded that it was best if they simply didn't know.

The eight young students followed the cobblestone trail up the hill from the docks, and on toward the mansion. Here and there along the path, antique-style street lamps mounted on low iron posts were already flickering with light, even though it was not yet fully dark. The posts were generously spaced; in fact they were set so far apart that the path would only be partly illuminated at night. Each was close enough to its neighbor to be easily seen, but not so close that their lights intermingled. Once the sun had vanished completely and the twilight deepened, the route from the docks to the mansion would slowly transform from a single winding path, into a dozen or more dim pools of light, each separated from the others by near-total darkness.

And equally peculiar to the lights' spacing was the inconsistency of their brightness. As the students made their way up the hill, the light nearest to them would grow noticeably more dim, though it would not go out entirely, while the next light further up the hill would seem to grow brighter, only to fade as soon as someone approached.

The net effect was, for want of a better word, "spooky".

But as the sun was not yet fully down, and ample twilight lingered, the students had no difficulty finding their way up the hill. Walking a bit ahead of the others, Monroe Jeffers – a European History major – stepped off the path to examine one of the streetlamps more closely.

"What is it?" asked Shelby, who was not far behind him.

"I'm trying to figure out what's up with these lights," Monroe replied. He hopped into the air a few times, craning his neck as far as he could, trying to get a closer look at the lamp itself.

"Motion sensors..." said Meri. "Pretty simple. They activate when we get close."

"Yeah, but why do they get darker? When we get close, shouldn't they light up *more*?"

"Maybe they're not so much to light up the path, but to show us where to go next," guessed Rodney.

"Oooooo... they're like will-o-the-wisps...!" said Liza, who had just caught up to the others.

"What?"

"Will-o-the-wisps..." she repeated ominously, putting her hands against her cheeks and playfully pretending to be scared. "Evil spirits... mysterious lights that float around in the darkness, and lead unwary travellers to their *doooom*."

Lizabel Paquero was a Religious Studies major, with an emphasis on archaic and pre-industrial cultures. She had a deep personal fascination for all things mysterious or spiritual, coupled with a profound intellectual cynicism for any sort of superstitious mumbo-jumbo. She managed to cope with these contradictory aspects of her worldview by never quite taking herself seriously.

"What are you talking about?" said Monroe again.

"They were in the reading, but I guess you didn't bother."

"I must have missed that week."

"Or like angler fish!" said Shondra, jumping into the discussion. "They're the ones that have that little light that dangles in front of their mouth to lure in prey. It's the same principle."

"Not to spoil the fun, but maybe they're just broken," Carson suggested. "A bad sensor could do that. Occam's Razor, kids."

Carson smiled broadly, as he often did at his own imagined display of expertise. The others let the conversation drop, and the group continued on up the hill toward the mansion.

The island of Doctor Grimdeath was a rocky and isolated patch of about one hundred and fifty acres, situated near the center of Lake Panasquana, some four or five miles from the mainland. In terms of its topography, it resembled nothing so much as a lumpy deflated balloon, or a wadded-up tan and green dishtowel, thrown carelessly onto the blue kitchen linoleum of the water.

The island was nearly circular in shape, and at its highest point the land rose some 100 feet above the surrounding lake. Waterfowl nested along the shoreline there, wherever they could find suitable cover, and many other birds inhabited the wooded areas further in. But aside from squirrels and mice and an occasional snapping turtle, no other animals were native to the place.

Apart from the jagged shoreline, and the lawns and gardens in the immediate vicinity of the mansion, most of the island's terrain consisted of light brushy forest, with a few well-maintained but unmarked walking trails meandering here and there. It should be noted that the island's forest contained no small number of formidable and ancient trees, but the stony, sandy ground prevented them from reaching any great height before they would topple over in the wind. It was the more patient and methodical trees – those that spread themselves wide, with sprawling roots and thick heavy trunks – which fared better than those that tried to grow too tall.

As the students drew closer to the house at the top of the hill, they could not help but be impressed. It was a large and imposing mansion, built in the Victorian Gothic style. Everything about it – from the asymmetrical facade with one tall octagonal turret, to the broad and columned front porch, to the deeply set double front doors, to the darkly shuttered windows – simply screamed with brooding atmosphere, and the sinister promise of what forbidden mysteries might be lurking inside.

"Cooooool..." muttered Rodney, quietly giving voice to the thoughts of everyone in the group.

"I wonder when this place was built," Monroe pondered aloud.

"Recently, I think," Shondra said. "As I understand it, there wasn't anything here at all until Doctor G bought the whole island, back whenever that was."

"Yah..." Liza agreed. "But who really knows? You can never be sure of anything from the stories around campus. It's hard to sort out truth from the legends half the time."

The students made their way up to the front porch, where they found a large, neatly hand-painted sign hanging from an iron hook on one of the doubled front doors. The sign read:

For your own safety!
Please do not knock on the door
or attempt to ring the doorbell.
Once your entire group is present, you may
proceed inside and wait in the grand foyer until
8:00 pm
at which time, you will receive further instructions.
Thank you for your compliance.

– Doctor Alistair Grimdeath

"Why would it be dangerous to ring the doorbell?" Rodney wondered aloud. But his question went unanswered.

"Eight o'clock..." mused Carson, pensively. "We aren't late are we? What time is it now?"

"Who knows?" said Meri, bitterly. "The Count of Quasimodo took all our phones and smartwatches."

"Surely we aren't late," said Monroe. "If we are it's the boat's fault."

"We aren't late," said Rodney, who was apparently the only member of the group that still wore an ordinary watch. "I have it as 7:54, give or take a minute."

"Well we're all here, right?..." Carson asked, as he demonstratively took a quick head count of the group. "Didn't lose anyone already, did we?" he joked, lamely. "Nope... seven, eight... We're all here. Shall we go in?"

Liza brushed past him without answering, and turned the ornate metal latch that opened the right-hand door. It swung silently open and she stepped inside, with the rest of the group filing in close behind her.

Chapter 4:
The Grand Foyer

Upon entering the mansion, the students found themselves standing in the spacious and elegant grand foyer. In the center of the room, a large Persian rug covered the hardwood floor, with a crystal chandelier hanging high above. An elegantly curving staircase swept up the righthand wall, leading to the second floor where a balcony overlooked the open area below. From both the upper story and the lower floor, doors and hallways could be seen, leading in all directions.

Some faint evening twilight filtered into the room from the curtained windows above and to either side of the main entry, but otherwise the foyer was only dimly lit from the high chandelier. There were candle sconces set here and there along the interior walls and underneath the balcony – eight of them in all – but their candles were all unlit.

To the immediate right of the entry doorway, a full suit of medieval armor was standing upright on a display pedestal, and to the opposite side a Grecian marble statue of a woman (or perhaps a goddess) was similarly situated. An enormous fireplace made of grey fieldstone dominated the left-hand side of the room, with a small metal rack of neatly stacked firewood standing beside it. Just above the fireplace mantle hung a large painting of a forested landscape underneath a full moon.

Near the foot of the staircase stood a tall grandfather clock. Its long pendulum could be seen through the glass-fronted door, slowly oscillating back and forth, making a quietly unobtrusive chik... chok... chik... chok... as the stopwork mechanism steadily advanced, and the hands of the clock inched slowly forward. It was 7:56.

"What a fabulous *room*...!" said Shelby, as she bounded forward into the foyer. She stopped abruptly at the edge of the Persian rug, where she thrust her arms out to either side, and began turning in slow, awestruck circles, trying to take it all in.

"It's nice, isn't it?" agreed Shondra, who was running her hand gently over the polished wooden rail of the staircase bannister. *"Really* nice... Doctor G does all right for himself on a college professor's salary."

"I've found the butler!" Carson announced, dramatically indicating the suit of armor that was standing beside the entry. "And the maid as well," he added, pointing to the marble statue. "I wonder if they'll take my jacket?"

"Keep it on," said Dean, who was standing in the center of the room, and looking wistfully over at the rack of kindling. "That's one hell of a fireplace, but I wish there was a fire in it; It's colder in here than it is outside."

Dean Rockwell was short, plump, and cheerfully good looking, if not classically handsome. He had a certain careless charm about him that made him seem familiar and welcoming, even to complete strangers. He was the sort of person that people would approach to ask for directions, if they were lost or couldn't find where they were going; it was something that happened to him fairly often, but he never seemed to mind.

Officially, his major was organic chemistry, but his real passion was for cooking, and sampling obscure international and ethnic cuisine. Once he'd completed his undergraduate degree, he planned to enter chef's school, and then to tour the world in search of unusual things to eat. The topic of food was rarely far from his mind.

"It *is* cold," Shelby agreed. "I can almost see my breath. I wonder if this place even has heat."

"Deliberate..." said Liza, cynically. "You can be sure there's central heating, but I'd take a bet that he turned it off, just for the final."

"I wouldn't put it past him," agreed Shondra.

As the other students wandered through the foyer, Rodney remained standing just inside the front entry doors, looking over the elegantly spacious room in much the same way that he might have looked at a large and unfamiliar dog whose friendliness was still in doubt. He was already feeling an urgent desire to simply get things over with.

"I assume *someone* is eventually going to tell us what we're supposed to be doing," he said, half-heartedly.

As if in direct response to Rodney's comment, the striking mechanism inside the grandfather clock made a quietly churning sound, as it suddenly came to life and began to chime the hour. It rang out with perfect precision, in stately and solemn tones, so slowly that an eternity seemed to pass between each stroke and the next. The students froze in place wherever they were, each of them in a different part of the room, to listen.

One...

Two...

Three...

"Aaaannnd, now it's eight o'clock." said Carson, needlessly.

Four...

Five...

Six...

Seven...

Eight.

The mechanism whirred to a stop, and the slow, relentless, *chik... chok...* of the clock's pendulum could be heard once again. The students stood in breathless suspense, intently listening, uncertain of what was to happen next.

"Here we go," said Dean suddenly, and with some relief. He pointed above the fireplace, and the others turned just in time to see the large painting which had been hanging there slide its way up along the wall to reveal a large flat-panel video display. The sound of a single violin could be very faintly heard, playing a haunting melody, somewhere in the distance. Everyone waited.

At first the screen was totally dark, but a few moments later it came silently to life. The following text was displayed there, in simple block lettering:

Dume University

Spring Semester

General Seminar 479, sections A-D

Welcome to your final exam

"PowerPoint..." grumbled Meri. "That's a let-down; I would have expected something like a video conference, at the very least."

"Cool background music, though..." whispered Shondra. "I can't even tell where it's coming from. Neat effect."

Rodney turned away from the screen for a moment to look up toward the balcony, more than half-expecting the professor to suddenly appear there. It was a reasonable suspicion – Doctor G had a flair for the dramatic – but aside from the eight students there was still no one else anywhere to be seen. It appeared that they were entirely alone.

"Next slide please," muttered Liza, quietly to herself. Standing only a few feet away, Shelby overheard her, and had to stifle a giggle.

A few seconds later, the text on the video screen did indeed change:

Semester Final:
Practical Application of Course Materials
Allotted Time: 12 Hours
(100 total points possible)
Students will be evaluated on their
completion of the following three items:

Then it changed again:

Part One: (25 points)
Identify the Monster

Part Two: (25 points)
Destroy the Monster

Part Three: (50 points)
Survive the Night

Collaboration among students
is permitted but not required.

Each of the students read and re-read these instructions several times. In the silence of the room, the grandfather clock's ticking seemed somehow louder than before.

Chapter 5:
The Debate

"OK..." said Meri, glaring at the video monitor. "What the *hell* does that mean?"

"What!?..." said Liza, feigning shock and outrage, "no multiple choice? No true/false? No short essay?..."

"There's obviously not a real monster..." said Carson, who didn't sound half as certain about it as he'd intended.

The group fell silent again for a few moments, waiting for the next slide, but it didn't come. The text on the screen didn't change. Rodney quietly shuffled a few steps backwards, putting himself out of view from the rest of the group, and took a long swig from his water bottle. He swallowed hard.

"That can't be all of it," said Meri.

"Typical PowerPoint," said Liza. "The presentation's hung."

"Me too," said Carson.

A few more seconds passed, but the text on the screen remained exactly as before.

"I get it..." said Dean, raising his hand in the air, as if he were hoping to be called on in class. "It's like an escape room."

"A what?"

"An escape room," Dean repeated. "I did one my sophomore year, with the Culinary Club. They lock you in, and you have to solve all kinds of different puzzles to get out."

"I've always wanted to do one of those," said Shondra, "but I never have. How'd it go?"

"It was a lot of fun," said Dean, "but... um... we didn't get out. The puzzles were really hard; we ran out of time."

"Well, that's encouraging," said Liza.

"Ok... so where does that leave us?" asked Shelby, who was determined to steer the conversation in a more productive direction. "That means we search the house and stuff, right?"

"Look for clues," said Dean, nodding affirmatively. "That'd be my guess, anyway."

"That's gonna feel weird," said Meri. "Going through somebody's closets and everything? Eeewww..."

"But that's the whole point, though," said Monroe. "I think Dean hit the nail on the head. I mean, why else would The Professor bring us out here? This place has probably all been set up, specifically for this. That's obviously what he expects us to do."

"Or we could stand here all night, waiting for our lemon-soaked paper napkins," suggested Liza.

It was at this moment that a set of previously inactive synapses made sudden contact inside Rodney's freshly lubricated brain, and his eyes lit up with the eager rush of epiphany.

"IT'S A MOVIE!!!" he shouted, a bit too loudly, startling everyone.

"Aaahh!..." exclaimed Meri, as she turned to glare at Rodney. "Don't *do* that."

"Don't you get it?" continued Rodney, undaunted. "It's so totally meta!... I mean, it's the classic movie set-up. Eight strangers trapped on a mysterious island with a mad scientist, with no phones, no contact with the outside world, and then a monster starts killing everybody. So the final exam, it's a movie, but instead of us watching it, we're inside it, right? So it's a *practicum*. It even said that on one of the slides, didn't it? So it's all the stuff we've been studying, but in application, not theory: *Survive the night*. Get it?"

"Yes, Rodney," said Shondra dryly, "we get it."

"You know, I wouldn't be a bit surprised if Doctor G really is filming all of this," said Meri. "Tiny little hidden cameras and what-not? I mean, how else could he grade us, if he's not here himself? I'd bet this whole place is wired for sound and video."

"So if it's a movie," said Dean, "who gets to be the hero?"

"Carson of course," said Liza. "Who else?"

"Oh me, I'll take that job," said Carson, pointing to himself demonstratively. "This is right up my alley. It's a role I was born to play."

"OK..." said Shelby, who was still trying to return the focus to the most relevant task at hand. "About the monster..."

"Yeah," said Meri. "That bothers me. What's up with that?"

"Well it's metaphorical, obviously," said Monroe. "Well, no, that's not right. Not metaphorical..."

"Hypothetical?..." suggested Shondra. "Theoretical?... Imaginary?..."

"Exactly.   That's what I meant.   Thank you," Monroe replied, gesturing in Shondra's direction. "It's obviously hypothetical. I mean, seriously... It's like war games in the military. They do this kind of thing all the time. Everyone operates exactly like they would in the real situation: troop movements, positional advantage, logistics, all of that. But you don't use real bullets; nobody really gets killed. So this is like... a monster attack *drill*. It's a test. Obviously. Doctor G wants us to demonstrate how well we're able to handle a simulated monster engagement."

"I feel like I should point out that if it's *not* theoretical," said Liza, bluntly, "then we are all in very deep shit."

"Come on," said Monroe. "Be serious."

"I *am* serious," said Liza. "Totally."

"Get real," said Monroe, dismissively. "You don't believe that nonsense for a minute."

"Did we even take the same class?" argued Liza. "Because I feel like you're missing something important here."

"I hope it is real," said Shelby, to the surprise of everyone else in the room. "Cause that would be *awesome*... We figure out what it is, we track it down, and then we kick its evil ass. I am *in*. Go team!"

This was a side of Shelby's personality that the others had seen only glimpses of over the course of the semester, and it caught them off-guard. For a moment, no one seemed to know quite what to say next.

"You do realize that's not how these things go, don't you?" said Liza, after a pause. "I mean, we're the underdogs here."

"Look... it doesn't matter," said Shondra, who could see that the group was already approaching an impasse.

"What do you mean it doesn't matter?" said Meri, who was liking this situation less and less.

Shondra sure as hell didn't believe that there would actually be a monster, but she also didn't see any point in wasting time arguing about it.

"It doesn't change what we're supposed to do," she explained. "Either way, monster or no monster, we've still got to figure out what it is, or what it's supposed to be, before we can do anything else about it. I think we should split up and take a look around."

"Um... I would like to call attention to the fact that just surviving the night is worth a full fifty points..." said Rodney, gesturing toward the display screen. "That's as much as the other two items *combined*."

"And fifty out of a hundred is still a failing grade," Shelby reminded him.

"We can't split up," insisted Rodney. "That's what always happens! The group splits up, and then the monster picks everybody off one by one. I think we should all stick together."

"So that way it can kill us all at once, right?" said Liza. "Nope, thanks. I'll take my chances."

"We obviously can't stick together," said Monroe. "Because if we do, we'll just keep arguing, and then we'll never get anywhere. I'm with the girls; we should split up and start searching the house in a thorough and systematic fashion."

Seeing himself heavily outvoted, Rodney crossed his arms and scowled, but didn't say anything further in reply.

Meri turned back to check the video monitor, which still hadn't changed.

"I dunno, guys, but it looks to me like this is all the guidance we're gonna get," she said.

There was a long, uncomfortable silence.

"Is anybody else hungry?" asked Dean, brightly. "If this is turning into an all-nighter, we've gotta have some munchies. I'm gonna go find the kitchen. Who wants pancakes?"

As the debate in the foyer drew to a close, the evening glow outside grew more and more dim. The last vestiges of twilight were fading, and giving way to night and the approaching storm.

As darkness consumed the forest, something unnatural there awakened, and slowly set itself into motion. Its shadow moved with it, as shadows have been known to do, while it made its way silently through the underbrush, drawing ever closer to the pale gleam of electric light that shone from the tall windows of the great house at the top of the hill.

Chapter 6:
Plan B

Outside the mansion, the wind was up, and a light rain was falling. Though occasional rumbles of thunder could be clearly heard in the distance, it seemed that the main storm had either missed the island entirely, or perhaps it was still yet to arrive. In the gathering gloom, there was no way to be certain.

Rodney pulled the hood up on his jacket as he made his way through the darkness, back down the cobblestone path toward the boat dock. He went as quickly as he could manage, hurrying from one lamp-post to the next, his eyes constantly adjusting as he transitioned from lamplight to shadow and back into light again. Not surprisingly, he strayed off the narrow pathway more than once, and often stumbled on the uneven surface of the ground. He was about halfway down the hill when he took his first real tumble, and landed with a thump in a patch of wet grass.

He lay there for a few moments, catching his breath and getting his bearings. Satisfied that he was uninjured – just a little dirtier and a little soggier than he'd already been – he stood up, shook himself off as best he could, then continued down the path a bit more slowly and cautiously than before.

"Get a grip," he mumbled to himself. "Haunted house... monster movie... don't want to be the idiot that gets drunk and panics and dies in the first fifteen minutes."

It should be said that Rodney was not drunk, at least not yet. He'd taken a few solid pulls at his water bottle, yes, but even that was not quite enough to fully fortify him against the rain and the swirling wind, and not nearly enough to muddle his thinking. In fact, for all he could tell, he was the only one of the group that was thinking clearly. If everybody else wanted to go wandering around inside the mansion looking for monsters, fine.

"Go for it," he muttered to himself, cynically. "Knock yourselves out."

But as for himself, Rodney had other plans. *Survive the night* sounded like a good idea to him, and he was determined to do just that.

Rodney was a Math major, and he had already worked out the most essential computation. There was no denying Shelby's observation that fifty points out of one hundred still amounted to a failing grade. But that would only mean an F for the final exam, and a fairly *high* F at that. Combining that with whatever points he'd earned over the course of the semester – and he was pretty sure he'd been pulling a low to mid-range B to that point – Rodney figured fifty percent on the final exam would still be enough to net him a high D or a low C for the course as a whole. That might not be anything to brag to his friends and family about, but it would still be a passing grade.

So with that calculus firmly in mind, Rodney figured all he really needed to do was to get his skinny ass safely off the island. The charter yacht wouldn't return to pick them all up until morning, and he knew he couldn't *swim* the five miles to shore, not even on a warm summer day in good weather, and certainly not on a chilly spring night in a rainstorm. But Rodney suspected there might yet be another way.

Back at the dock in the little sheltered cove, he found exactly what he was looking for. He was sure he'd remembered seeing a storage shed of some sort beside the pier when the boat first brought them to the island, and there it was, in all its dilapidated glory.

"There *is* a boathouse," Rodney said aloud, "I knew there was."

He stood there for a moment at the end of the cobblestone path, catching his breath, and giving himself a little congratulatory fist pump.

"Well done, Rodney," he said with a smile. "Score."

The shed sat alongside the dock, only a few yards from the water's edge. The near corner of the building was faintly illuminated by the last lamp post, which stood at the foot of the long wooden pier. From his vantage point, Rodney couldn't see any sort of door or entrance, though there was a small four-paned window on the shack's inland wall. He walked up to it and looked in.

There wasn't enough light for him to see anything inside the shed clearly, but he thought he could make out a large, dark shape that looked very much like it might be some sort of boat, covered by a sheet or a tarpaulin.

Rodney's heart began to beat a little bit faster, and he hurried around the corner of the building, looking for a way inside. What he found was a set of double doors, which took up almost the entirety of the building's end wall. He tried to pull them open, but it was no good; they were held with a metal clasp, and securely padlocked shut.

Rodney's heart sank. He didn't have the key, obviously, nor any other way to open the padlock or break into the shed. He walked back to the window and peered inside again. There was definitely a boat underneath that tarp; he was sure of it. He stepped back, and took a moment to collect his thoughts and decide what to do.

"I can't get in there without tools," he muttered to himself, "and that boat's too big, anyway. I'd probably need help just to get it out to the water."

He frowned, and turned to look back up the dimly lit path toward the mansion.

"Ok," he said aloud, resigning himself to this temporary setback. "Important piece of information: there's a boat if we need it. So we'll go back up the hill and see if anybody else has learned anything useful yet. Right... This sounds like a plan."

Chapter 7:
Plan A

It seemed to Shondra that the most sensible approach to exploring the mansion was to first make a quick survey of the ground floor, starting at the grand foyer then moving systematically from room to room to ensure that nothing was overlooked. Once that was done, a more careful search could proceed in those places that seemed most likely to yield fruitful results.

But predictably enough, everyone else had their own ideas, and they'd scattered to the four winds, guided either by impulse, or intuition, or some other potentially faulty rationale. But Shondra had a plan, and she had every intention of sticking with it until she came upon a damned good reason not to.

She took the first door on the right-hand side of the foyer, and found herself standing in a little room that looked out toward the mansion's side lawn. At first glance, it appeared to be some sort of sitting room or breakfast nook. For simplicity's sake, she mentally catalogued it as *The Parlor*.

If the foyer felt impressive and intimidating, this little room felt charming, even inviting, and positively cozy. Several upholstered armchairs were comfortably spaced here and there, with side tables and footstools appropriately arranged. A cloth-covered tea cart was tucked neatly into one corner, with crisply folded napkins and silver spoons and a complete blue and white china tea service, all clean and spotless and at the ready. The teapot, however, was empty; there was no tea. Shondra didn't see anything that looked strange, or out of the ordinary, aside from the fact that the whole room seemed almost impossibly quaint, as if it were really just for show, and not a space that was ever actually used.

She pulled a curtain back, and looked out to the side yard. There was a little white gazebo there, standing all by itself, about halfway between the mansion and the trees. It was faintly illuminated by a single electric light that hung from the center of its roof, leaving most of the lawn in shadow. In the misty rain, it had an almost ethereal glow.

Shondra stood there for some time, looking out that window at the little gazebo. There was something about it that she found unaccountably fascinating. Maybe it was just the ambiance of the rain-spattered window, and that one lonely beacon of light calling out from the surrounding darkness. Or maybe there was something else... She had the strangest sense of deja vu, as if it was reminding her of something that she couldn't quite put her finger on... She just wasn't sure.

"Maybe I should sneak out there for a quick look, before the rain gets any worse," she thought, though she was already shaking her head to tell herself "no". She knew it was a bad idea, though she did feel sorely tempted.

Then the moment passed, as something else caught her eye and broke the reverie. On the far side of the yard, beyond the gazebo and near the edge of the trees, Shondra thought she had glimpsed someone moving through the shadows. She looked again, but she couldn't be certain. The window glass was covered with a fine spray of water droplets, making it difficult to see anything clearly. It might have been only a tree branch moving in the wind.

Shondra let the curtain fall back into place, and stepped away from the window. She told herself that she was getting a little too wrapped up in the spirit of the exercise, and consequently making things out to be even spookier than they already were. She brushed it off.

"This is kind of fun," she said aloud, although she didn't entirely believe it.

Only a few steps down one of the hallways from the foyer, Monroe Jeffers discovered the mansion's billiard room. It was a squarish, windowless chamber with a rather high ceiling, well-lit from overhead and from various smaller fixtures mounted along the room's outer walls.

The massive and immaculately carved pool table stood in the room's precise center, surrounded by high wooden stools and several tall chairs that afforded a good view of the playing surface. A single rack along the right-hand wall held perhaps a dozen top-quality cue sticks, each of them uniquely adorned with intricate inlays made from various exotic species of wood. Hanging on the left-hand wall was a simple slate chalkboard where players would presumably tally the scores of their games, while at the far end of the room stood a sizable liquor cabinet, mounted on the wall behind a standing bar.

Monroe considered himself a reasonably competent billiards player; he'd often played as a child, as his uncle had a table in his house. Monroe had even won a few dollars here and there in casual games with friends in some of the bars near the Dume University campus. He took one of the cue sticks down from the rack and studied it, more out of admiration for the quality of its craftsmanship than from any real intention to play.

At first glance, it appeared that the table had already been set up for a game of nine-ball, but looking more closely, Monroe saw that there were in fact only *eight* balls on the table. They were neatly racked together in a traditional diamond configuration, but with the nine-ball inexplicably absent, leaving the top of the diamond lopped off.

Monroe made a quick search of the table's side and corner pockets, but the missing ball was nowhere to be found. Nor could he locate the numberless white cue ball, or the other striped balls that would normally have been numbered from ten to fifteen. He did find an empty case, which had apparently once held the complete set, but search as he might, there seemed to be no other balls anywhere in the room, aside from those that were already so neatly arranged on the table.

As the other students scattered in various directions, Dean remained in the grand foyer to try and see if he could get a fire going in the fireplace. The wood that was stored in the kindling rack was dry and well-seasoned, and did not seem to be there simply for show. By all appearances, it had been put there with the expectation that it would actually be used.

Dean thought back to his earlier experience with the escape room, and wondered if lighting the fireplace might be a necessary step in solving some as-yet-undiscovered puzzle that Doctor G had concocted for them. But even if not, there was still the practical consideration that it was uncomfortably cold in the house, and having a nice warm fire in a central location would probably stand to benefit everyone, even if it didn't have any direct bearing on them completing their final exam.

To Dean's considerable disappointment, no one else in the group had shared his interest in pancakes, or in any other type of quick and easy-to-prepare snack food. In fact, no one else seemed to have any interest in food at all, and his enthusiastic suggestion had been quickly rejected in no uncertain terms. He'd let the matter drop, telling himself that he'd try again sometime later in the evening. Perhaps after the initial excitement wore off, the others would be more inclined to give a little attention to matters of simple practicality, like eating and keeping warm.

When most other people got excited, they couldn't be bothered to even think about food. But when Dean got excited, food was usually the first thing he thought about. No matter the circumstances, he had to have the sustenance situation well under control before he could be at his best. His brain simply couldn't function at its peak capacity without an adequate fuel supply; this was something Dean understood about himself very well, from long personal experience. He was never more relaxed or focused than when he was comfortably well-fed.

He found a small stash of kitchen matches stored inside a little copper box on the mantlepiece, and some old newspapers tucked into a sleeve on the side of the kindling rack. He took a moment to scan the headlines, but they appeared to be just ordinary local papers from one of the small towns that bordered on the lake. Once he was satisfied that he wouldn't be accidentally burning up some vital clue, Dean soon had a nice little blaze going, and in its comforting glow the grand foyer soon felt much more welcoming and secure.

With his first task accomplished, Dean departed the foyer, and moved further into the mansion's interior. No matter what the others thought, this was a personal quest for him, and he would not be dissuaded.

He was determined to find the kitchens.

———————————

Carson wasn't worried about monsters or any other sort of danger that might be lurking, either inside the mansion or on the island outside. He'd already figured it all out. Something Meri had said back in the foyer had suddenly brought the whole situation into perfect focus for him, and the more he thought about it, the more confident he became.

That geek Rodney had said that the whole thing was like a movie, but it was Meri's comment that cut to the heart of the matter. It wasn't *like* a movie, it *was* a movie... a movie with an audience of one: Doctor Grimdeath himself. This was, after all, their final exam. He'd have to give them a grade, and that grade would be based on how they performed on the fly, under pressure, and without any rehearsal.

This was something Carson could wrap his head around. He wasn't as good as some of the others at the research and the history and the lab work and the ancient languages, but he knew how to put on a good performance, and sell a few hours of compelling dramatic action. He was already certain, without any shadow of a doubt, that this was going to be his greatest performance.

He had not yet realized that it would also be his last.

Carson didn't have any particular plan for how to go about looking for clues or monsters; he just chose a direction that no one else seemed to be going, and let fate be his guide.

As it turned out, fate led him to the Trophy Room.

The Trophy Room was a large, formally arranged gentleman's lounge, lovingly furnished in the testosterone-laden style of 19th century European colonial sporting machismo. When Carson first opened the door, the only light – aside from what spilled in from the hallway – came from a single standing floor lamp. The harshly contrasting shadows made the place seem even more disturbing than it would already have been.

Above and to either side of the fireplace, were mounted antique weapons of all sorts, ranging from a Zulu spear and war shield, to a pair of Amazonian blowguns, to an English halberd, to a Prussian cavalry sabre. There was even a matched set of dueling pistols, tucked neatly away in a glass display case along with a brass powderhorn and a variety of other small trinkets that Carson could not immediately identify. But of all the old weapons on display, pride of place had been given to a large, slightly rusty and very old-looking blunderbuss, which hung directly above the fireplace mantle. It was apparently an item greatly prized.

The rest of the room was something like a taxidermist's fashion show. In one corner stood a large and snarling Kodiak bear, while on a display pedestal opposite was a black leopard, poised in a low crouch, as if it were ready to spring at any moment. The walls of the room were almost completely covered with the stuffed heads of large and very dead animals, all mounted on wooden plaques. There were dozens of them, and though many of the specimens were familiar – an African lion, a Thompson's gazelle, a timber wolf, and so on – many were not.

Carson felt strangely uneasy, looking around the room at all the dead animals. Illuminated from below, as they were, their mounted heads threw haunting, sinister shadows along the walls and onto each other. Carson could not shake off the unpleasant sensation that these creatures were watching him, judging him, and warning him to go no further. He could even hear in the distance – or imagined that he could – the slow, ominous rhythm of tribal drums.

He spotted a light switch beside the door, and flipped it on. The shadows instantly vanished, and the drumbeats fell silent. Taking a second look around the room, Carson suddenly laughed out loud in spite of himself.

He hadn't noticed it at first, but now with better light he could clearly see that one of the trophy heads was a unicorn. It was obviously a fake, or so he assumed, though a fairly convincing one all the same.

"Got me!" he said aloud, playing it up for the hidden cameras that he assumed must be watching him from somewhere inside the room. He pointed at the unicorn head with both hands, winked conspiratorially, and gave his cheesiest grin.

"But it will take more than that to scare *Carson McBride!*" he added.

His delivery was a little awkward, and not as convincing as he would have liked, but it was the most heroic-sounding line that Carson could come up with under the circumstances.

Chapter 8:
The Upper Story

As the other students explored the ground floor, Liza and Meri decided to start with the upper story, and then work their way down from there. They climbed the staircase together, but parted ways when they reached the top: Meridian going to the right, and Lizabel to the left.

The balcony above the foyer was part of a long, continuous hallway that led to all the various rooms of the mansion's second floor. The corridor formed a complete loop, so that someone walking along it – after navigating a complicated sequence of blind turns both left and right – would eventually end up right back where they started.

Though the hallway was reasonably wide, and equipped with electric lighting fixtures, for anyone unaccustomed to the place it still felt cramped and darkly claustrophobic. This was because, aside from the high balcony with its open view of the grand foyer, the hallway's many twists and turns made it impossible to ever see very far along it in any one direction.

Making her way slowly down that corridor, the only thing Liza felt certain about was the fact that she couldn't feel certain about anything. The more rational, more logical, more domesticated part of her brain assured her that there wasn't really going to be a monster, or even anything genuinely dangerous. This was only a test; a role-playing exercise; just one more bit of unnerving weirdness at the end of what had been a weirdly unnerving and unreasonably difficult class.

But it bears mentioning that Liza's brain was not fully domesticated. In fact, she had over the last several years invested a great deal of time and effort into *peeling back* the layers of domestication that society had long tried to impose on her. She had not merely gotten in touch with her inner psyche, she'd invited it over for tea and crumpets then had wildly passionate sex with it on the hallway carpet. Ever since, she and her own primal nature had settled into what could best be described as a modestly stable, if somewhat tempestuous, long-term relationship. It seemed to be working out reasonably well for the both of them.

That was, after all, why Liza had signed up for this class in the first place. She had thought it would be the perfect opportunity for a focused exploration of the very subjects she'd already been experimenting with on her own, only with the expert guidance of an acknowledged master of the medium. It seemed like a good idea at the time.

But now, not so much. Whether she and her fellow students were really in immediate physical danger, or if that danger was merely hypothetical or psychological, Liza had long since arrived at the uncomfortable suspicion that she and the others were no longer Professor Grimdeath's students. Instead, they had now become – and perhaps had already been since the start of the semester – his test subjects.

One of the first things Meri noticed about the upstairs hallway was how poorly lit it was. The antique electric fixtures along the walls weren't terribly bright, but even so they should have provided ample illumination, except for the fact that they were so poorly arranged. They all seemed to be placed near the hallway corners, but on the *inside* of the turns, so that rather than shining in all directions, they instead threw steep and angular shadows up and along the surface of the walls, making it far more difficult to judge distances, or to see anything clearly.

Eager to get out of the moodily-lit hallway, Meri stopped at the first door she came to. She tapped on it lightly, more out of polite habit than any real concern that there might be someone else in the room. Hearing no reply to her timid knocking, she slowly turned the knob, cracked the door open ever so slightly, and peered cautiously inside.

It was a bedroom, modestly-sized and tastefully furnished in the same antique style as the foyer had been. A simple four-poster bed dominated the far side of the space, with a chair and a writing desk beside a large curtained window. The overhead light was already on, making the room seem far more bright and cheerful than the shadowy upstairs hall. She swung the door open the rest of the way, and stepped into the room.

Standing there, Meri could almost feel the tension in her shoulders dissolving. The white lace curtains hanging at the window; the blue and white coverlet on the bed; the ocean-blue rug on the hardwood floor, all made the room feel comforting, familiar, and secure. It had the sort of atmosphere that Meri might have expected to find in a charming little bed and breakfast somewhere in the Berkshires. It was elegant and tasteful, with all of its antique charm intact. This was her kind of place.

Liza had already guessed that the upstairs hallway formed a complete loop, and she thought she must be roughly halfway around it when she came to a large set of double doors.

She'd not investigated any of the other rooms she'd come past to that point; she'd wanted to confirm the layout of the hallway before venturing further. But whatever room these doors led to was clearly important, and too enticing for her to simply pass on by without a closer look. She reached out, grasped a brass knob in each hand, pushed the doors gently open, and found herself gazing in at a vast and astonishing library.

The floor was covered in deep red carpet, patterned with an ornate black and gold design. Three large reading tables were set in different parts of the room, with various easy chairs, end tables, floor lamps, and even a lounge settee neatly scattered throughout the space. There were several glass-topped display cabinets as well, and the walls were completely lined with tall bookcases reaching from floor to ceiling, each of them packed with books of all sizes and descriptions.

Just from where she was standing, Liza could see everything from ancient leather-bound tomes to modern mass-market paperbacks, all chaotically shelved without any visible system of organization. The effect was something like a deranged fantasy of an otherworldly used book store, brought impossibly to life, directly from some mad bibliophile's most passionate nightmare.

This was more than she was prepared to tackle at the moment. Even at first glance, Liza could see that this was a room that might take hours to explore, just to make a cursory scan for any obvious hints Professor Grimdeath might have planted there.

She very quietly closed the doors again, and stood there for a moment collecting her thoughts. Then suddenly she felt herself shuddering, and realized that she'd broken out in a cold sweat.

Meri sat on the edge of the four-poster bed and bounced up and down on it a few times, running her hands over the quilted coverlet. She found herself wishing she could forget all about the exam, and just snuggle in for a good night's sleep. But there wasn't time for that, of course. She sighed and stood up, and took another look around the room to see if there was anything there that looked like it might be some sort of clue.

The closet.

She'd overlooked it before, but for some reason, now the closet door had caught her interest. What might be in there? She wondered.

Nothing else in the room seemed at all out of the ordinary. There was nothing on the writing table: no half-written letter or unfinished snifter of brandy; no partially-burned photograph, nor any of the other sorts of things that always seemed to be found on writing tables in the horror films and mystery novels that they'd studied over the course of the semester. She even stooped down to check underneath the bed, but found nothing there other than the hardwood flooring and the carpet.

That left only the closet.

As she reached out to open the closet door, she felt a sudden and inexplicable wave of apprehension wash over her. She froze in place, her hand still several inches from the burnished doorknob, as if some latent instinct or intuition of danger were holding her back.

She stepped away from the door, and carefully looked it over from top to bottom. But she could see nothing odd about it. It was a dark, paneled wooden door, just like all the other doors in the house. It wasn't as if there was some sort of creepy, otherworldly light coming from the cracks above or underneath or around the doorframe; there weren't any mysterious scratches on its surface, nor anything else overtly suspicious about the door at all, not so far as Meri could see.

And then she heard it... the strange melody. It was very faint, similar to the distant and haunting violin that Shondra had pointed out in the foyer, but sharper, more insistent. And not the sound of a single instrument, but a chorus of strings, just at the edge of hearing.

Dun... dun-duuuuun-dun-Dun!..... duunnnn....

She couldn't tell where the music was coming from, but as she approached the closet door again it seemed to grow louder, darker, more intense than before.

She could feel her heart racing. She wanted to flee; to escape the room; to run back down the stairs to the foyer; to find Liza, or Carson, or anyone else... but her feet would not obey, as if they were frozen in solid ice.

She watched as her own hand reached out toward the door, like a thing beyond her control. She tried to draw it away, but still it inched forward. Soon, she could feel the cold metal surface of the doorknob, as her fingers wrapped themselves around it and slowly began to turn.

The music seemed deafening now. Where were the others? Couldn't they hear the music? Why didn't they come? Why couldn't she stop her hand?

Unable to bear it any longer, Meri suddenly twisted the knob sharply, and yanked the closet door open wide.

Her screams echoed all along the upstairs hall.

Chapter 9:
Mismatch

Shelby Oswald was standing underneath a wide archway that opened into the formal dining room, wrestling with the uncomfortable suspicion that she and the others were going about this all wrong.

It was a nice house, there was no arguing that. It was richly nice; extravagantly, tastefully, jaw-droppingly nice. She was certain that she could wander through that house for days, and never get tired of it.

But they didn't have days. They had twelve hours at the very most; and if there really was a monster, they probably had far less time than that.

And *was* there really going to be a monster? The group hadn't reached any sort of consensus about it.

Shelby walked slowly through the room, only half-noticing the elegant furnishings. There was a long formal dining table, heavily built and ornately carved. Against the far wall stood an enormous glass-fronted china cabinet made of the same dark wood, and similarly polished to a fine lustre. The table had been set for eight with neatly folded white linen napkins and elegant porcelain dinnerware, though oddly there were no forks or knives, nor any similar utensils anywhere to be seen. A low vase with gold trim had been arranged as a centerpiece, holding a tidy cluster of small purple wildflowers.

Displayed inside the glass-fronted cabinet were additional cups, saucers, plates and serving bowls, all of the exact same design as those already on the table: a circlet of roses on a white background, with a single rose offset from the rest. Shelby did not know the name of the china pattern, but any dealer in fine antiques could have told her that it was called "Drop-Rose Haviland," and was still quite popular among collectors. Shelby was fond of antiques, and on any other day she might have been fascinated to learn every detail about the doctor's collection of fine old china. But for the moment, her mind was very much elsewhere. She ran a finger over the gleaming surface of the hardwood table, lost in her own thoughts.

As recently as six months before, Shelby would have found the mere suggestion of a bloodthirsty monster, or of any sort of supernatural creature, to be a laughable children's fantasy. But after spending the past semester intensely researching the mysteries of the arcane – both in ancient lore and modern practice – she was no longer nearly so certain.

But even if the monsters of myth and legend *weren't* real, she reasoned, by harnessing the full potential of modern science Doctor G might very well be able to *make* one, if he put his mind to it. After all, if Professor Alistair Grimdeath didn't match the classic definition of a mad scientist, no one did; and given what she'd learned of the man over the past few months, Shelby certainly wouldn't put it past him.

And that's when the realization hit her: *Mad scientists don't make monsters in the dining room.* Then where do they make them? In a laboratory. Or more precisely, in a **secret** laboratory.

The proverbial light bulb flickered on.

The dining room, the foyer, maybe the whole of the mansion was just a red herring. It was a distraction, like a magician's sleight of hand. If she wanted to find the monster, or at least to figure out what the monster was supposed to be, she had to find the secret laboratory where it would have been made.

That was it. She'd put her thumb on it at last. Shelby Oswald finally knew exactly what she was looking for.

She had to tell the others.

When Monroe Jeffers returned to the grand foyer, it was quiet and empty; no one else seemed to be around. A nice fire was burning in the fireplace, but otherwise nothing about the room seemed to have changed from before. He glanced over at the grandfather clock, and saw that it was now 8:41 pm.

Monroe was carrying his windbreaker in one hand, and a pool cue in the other. Working under the assumption that this was indeed supposed to be a simulated monster attack, he figured that the first order of business would be to suitably arm himself, and in Monroe's mind, a pool cue was the perfect weapon for the current exercise. It could plausibly make for an effective cudgel, if used like a quarterstaff or swung like a club, but it wasn't otherwise inherently dangerous. He had a strong suspicion that someone trying to carry around something like an old sword or a woodsman's axe, or even a sharp kitchen knife was more likely to injure themselves by accident than anything else. Now that he thought about it, Monroe wondered if that was why the professor had required everyone to sign that personal injury waiver, before the exam had even started.

But beyond the safety aspect, Monroe felt that the pool cue was a perfect choice of weapon because there was a suitably "improvised" feel to it. In all the movies and literature Doctor Grimdeath had forced the group to study over the course of the semester, it was a common feature that monsters were rarely, if ever, defeated by the use of conventional weaponry. Monroe suspected that this was an important detail, and that employing a more creative selection of armament might even earn him a few bonus points. It couldn't hurt.

He pulled his jacket back on, and leaned the cue against the stones of the fireplace, while he warmed himself in front of the fire. Walking around the mansion, he hadn't really noticed the cold, but loitering there in the foyer he'd begun to feel positively chilly again.

He was still standing there rubbing his hands together when Shelby appeared from one of the interior hallways.

"Where is everybody?" she asked.

"I have no idea," Monroe replied. "They're not here."

Shelby scowled and looked around the room impatiently. She'd hoped that more of the group would be here.

"Did you find anything interesting?" Monroe asked, more trying to make polite conversation than expecting that Shelby had actually made any significant progress on the exam assignment. It might be fair to say that Monroe seriously underestimated Shelby's intelligence. This had less to do with any inherent sexism or a misplaced reliance on stereotyping, than with a fundamental feature of Monroe's personality: he tended to underestimate everyone.

"I think..." Shelby started to reply, but hesitated. She knew Monroe wasn't likely to take her seriously, no matter what she had to say. She figured she'd have more success conferring with some of the others in the group instead.

Monroe gave Shelby a curious look and waited patiently for her to finish her sentence, but she didn't. The silence in the room had just begun to feel awkward, when they faintly heard a distant scream, coming from somewhere on the upper floor.

Chapter 10:
A Closet Case

Liza came crashing into the bedroom like an outside linebacker on a corner blitz, to find Meri still very much alive, but crumpled on the floor, taking deep breaths and wiping tears out of her eyes.

"Are you ok...?" Liza asked, puzzled. "What the hell...?"

"...scared..." was the only word Meri could muster. "...sorry..." she added a moment later, then raised a hand and pointed. "Closet... I'm ok."

The closet door was closed; Meri had apparently slammed it shut again, before falling to the floor. Liza looked the door over suspiciously, then took a step toward it just as Monroe and Shelby appeared in the hallway outside.

"Are you guys ok?" Shelby asked, panting for breath. "We heard a scream."

"Quiet!" Liza said sharply. She stood there listening intently for a moment, but heard only silence. There was no music, no other sound than her own breathing and that of her classmates. She turned back to face the closet door, but as she reached for the knob, she felt a presence... as if something evil were lurking there, hidden from sight.

Steeling her nerves, she cautiously pulled the door open again.

Liza wasn't sure what exactly she was expecting to find in that closet – a bloody corpse, a colony of spiders, a skeleton hanging from the light fixture – all of these possibilities and more had flashed through her mind. But whatever she'd expected, it wasn't a solid wall of pastel tuxedos.

But there they were. The hanging rack inside that bedroom closet was packed nearly to overflowing with hideous polyester tuxedos from the early 1970's: powder blue, mint green, salmon pink, soft lavender, and creamsicle orange. They dangled there silently, in pristine condition, complete with their viciously tapered slacks and white frilled dress shirts, their deeply pleated cummerbunds, and their wrinkle-free jackets with grotesquely outsized lapels.

"Hah?!... What the hell?..." said Monroe with a laugh.

"So *wrong*..." said Meri, who was finally getting ahold of herself again.

"Is this why you screamed?" asked Liza, incredulous.

"You didn't hear the music!" Meri replied, defensively. "And you were scared too; admit it."

Liza thought about it... she *had* been scared. And she'd felt something as well: Something discordant... something horribly out of place, or possibly even *evil*.

"Meri's right..." said Shelby, quite seriously. "This is wrong."

"Fashion crime: punishable by death," said Monroe.

"It's the wrong era," Shelby continued, as if she were trying to explain it to herself, but still didn't quite understand. "Everything else here is *old*, or looks old, but these are just... out of date?... I dunno."

"They sure as hell don't fit with the rest of the house," Liza agreed. "They're from the wrong time period, at the very least."

"And the wrong everything else," said Meri, bitterly.

"They *are* pretty horrifying, though," said Monroe, "so there's that."

"Why are you carrying a pool cue?" Liza asked. She'd just noticed that Monroe was holding a pool cue, and wondered why, exactly, he was carrying a pool cue. So she asked.

"Self-defense," Monroe replied. "Can't be too careful with these killer tuxedos roaming about."

"Wait a second..." said Shelby. She stepped past Liza into the closet doorway, and pushed the tuxedos to either side so she could see past them.

"That's it...!" she said, turning back to the group excitedly. "There's a whole room back here!"

Any remaining fear or confusion the four students might have felt was immediately swept away by the excitement of discovery. They set to work clearing the closet entrance, pulling the colorful tuxedos down off the rack and piling them (none too carefully) on the bed.

They soon discovered that the room behind the tuxedos was actually a spacious walk-in closet, nearly as large as the actual bedroom. Cabinets and shelves – mostly empty, aside from a few neatly stacked bed linens and bath towels – lined the walls. There were other clothes racks there as well, all completely empty. Seeing those, it was apparent to the four students that the tuxedos had been hung over the closet doorway deliberately to conceal the rest of the storage space, though why Professor Grimdeath would have wanted to keep this almost empty room hidden wasn't immediately obvious.

"There's a gap here," said Liza, looking closely at one of the wall-mounted cabinets. "I think I can see hinges..."

"It's another door," said Shelby, "good find! There's a latch on this side."

Shelby popped the metal catch, and the cabinet swung away from the wall a few inches. The hinges creaked only slightly as the four students pulled it the rest of the way open to reveal a hidden narrow corridor.

"A secret passageway," said Liza. "Now *this* is cool."

"It's cramped," said Meri, apprehensively. "Who goes first?"

"I'll go..." said Monroe, who considered himself the best qualified to take charge, now that the others had actually found something interesting. "Just follow me: I've got a pretty good guess what this is."

The tiny corridor was no more than a yard wide, but unlike the main second-story hallway it ran perfectly straight, and was not badly lit. They made their way down it cautiously, with Monroe in front, carrying his cue stick.

"This could be dangerous..." Liza pointed out, sarcastically. "Not enough room in here to swing your weapon of choice."

"Hah," said Monroe. "You think so? Look at this!"

He turned back to demonstrate, as he twisted the cue in the middle and it unscrewed into two pieces, leaving one half with a threaded metal peg and the other with an empty wooden socket.

"Impressed?" He said, proudly. "*High tech stuff.* You could almost hide this thing in a violin case, now."

Carrying half of his pool cue in each hand, Monroe led the group the rest of the way down the narrow corridor. It soon ended at another little room very like the one they'd just come from. Instead of bath-towels and bed-linens, however, this room had a large cupboard filled with glassware and other dishes, a few serving trays, and another shelf completely stacked with neatly folded napkins and tea towels. There was also a long work counter with a faucet and sink, and in another corner of the room was a good-sized dumbwaiter.

"As I thought," Monroe said. "This was a servants' corridor. Lots of these things in old mansions like this. It's so the hired help could get around without being noticed, or disturbing the guests. I'd bet we're standing right above the kitchens. That dumbwaiter might even go all the way down to the wine cellar."

"I think this is another door," Meri said, indicating a section of shelving that was outlined by a narrow seam. At first glance, it looked much like all the other cabinetry in the room, except that there was a simple latching mechanism, partially concealed under one of the middle shelves.

Although she'd been the one to find it, Meri was still feeling a little too shaken to take the lead, and was more than happy to take a step back and have someone else open up the wall panel first. Liza, however, was pretty sure she knew where this new door led to, and didn't hesitate to trip the latch. As the shelf swung open, her guess was confirmed, and the group found themselves looking in at the mansion's upstairs library.

"I thought so," Liza said with a nod. "It's a very cool library; I saw it from the other side. Those double doors over there lead back out into the main hallway."

Chapter 11:
Out of the Rain

"Damnit, damnit, damnit...! Now it's *really* coming down..."

Shondra was standing in the middle of the little white gazebo in the side yard, and cursing with disgust. She was cursing at the rain and she was cursing at her own rotten luck, but mostly she was cursing at her own stupidity: she should have known better.

In fact, she did know better; she'd had a perfectly good plan, and if she had stuck with it, she'd still be inside the mansion, and would probably be finishing up her exploration of the ground floor by now. But her curiosity had gotten the best of her. After taking a quick look around the parlor, she'd moved on to the other rooms of the ground floor, just as she'd planned. But after glancing through the kitchen, the dining room, and a couple of interior hallways, she'd gotten impatient, and a little bit bored. Everything looked the same. Professor Grimdeath's mansion was awash with antique elegance, but it looked more like a museum or a movie set than a place where anyone actually lived. It was all so spotless. No loose papers, no dirty dishes, not even a muddy footprint on the floor.

Well, there would damn well be some muddy footprints on the floor soon, if she had anything to say about it. But for the moment, she was stuck, unless she wanted to get thoroughly, thoroughly drenched. She didn't.

Ever since she'd first noticed it out the window of that little parlor room, Shondra had found that she couldn't stop thinking about the gazebo. She wasn't sure why. Maybe the isolation of it, this little shining glimmer of white, glowing in the darkness. Maybe it was the pure kitsch factor... gazebos have a certain unique charm, largely due to their very limited utility. But either way, it didn't matter now. For whatever the reason, she'd decided to suspend her investigation of the ground floor, and sneak a closer peek at the gazebo before it started raining any harder.

When she'd first dashed out the front entry, there was only a light sprinkle coming down... really not much more than a drizzle. But no sooner had she reached her destination than a huge clap of thunder shook the air, and the stormclouds broke open in an absolute deluge.

"This can't last," she told herself. "It's got to let up sometime. Damnit, girl... lesson learned. Stick with the plan, always, always, always... Damn. Damn it, god-damn it, damn..."

Even standing in the very center of the structure wasn't good enough to keep Shondra totally dry. The wind hadn't let up even a tiny bit, and it kept changing directions. No matter where she stood she couldn't avoid getting sprayed with the blowing rain now and again. But still, it was better than being out in the storm entirely unprotected. If she ran for the house now, she'd be a sodden rag by the time she got there, and it wasn't like she had a dry change of clothes with her.

She saw a light come on in a window at the rear corner of the main house. From what she'd learned about the general layout of the mansion, she guessed that one of the other students must have found the kitchen.

"Probably Dean," she said, shaking her head and smiling in spite of herself. "That boy wants his pancakes, and you can't stop a man on a mission. Damn. Go for it, son. You do you."

She kicked playfully at one of the puddles of water on the gazebo's concrete floor, took a deep breath of the chilly air and sighed, trying to decide whether to make the dash for the house, or if she should wait a little longer for the rain to let up.

And then she thought she heard music.

She looked up and strained to listen over the noise of the falling rain, and yes, she was sure of it now... it was the same lonely violin that she'd heard in the foyer, but that wasn't where she'd heard it first... then it came to her: it was the same tune that the boatman had been whistling on the charter yacht... she was sure of it. That couldn't just be a coincidence, but what did it mean?

Shondra still couldn't tell where the music was coming from, but it seemed to be getting louder. She could hear it clearly now, despite the sounds of the rain. She looked up and all around the frame of the gazebo to see if she could spot any wires or hidden speakers, though there was nothing there that she could see. But the music had to be coming from *somewhere*.

"Ok... where is that little beastie?" she asked herself. "Maybe it's waterproof... they can make those damn things so small these days."

She checked all around the porch railing, and even stepped out a little toward the edges of the structure to look up under the overhanging cornice of the roof. But with the rain and the darkness she could see nothing there other than neatly painted wood.

"Damn it, where is it?..." she asked in frustration.

As if in answer, something large and heavy crashed into Shondra from behind, knocking her down to the gazebo's wet concrete floor. Claws tore at her back and sides, as sharp fangs twisted at her neck, rending her throat and piercing deep into her windpipe.

By the time she thought to scream, it was too late. She was already dead.

Chapter 12:
One Down...

Rodney was standing just inside the main entry to the mansion, kicking off his muddy shoes and trying to shake the water off of his clothes and out of his hair.

It could have been much worse. He'd felt the wind picking up as the heavy rain got closer, but he nearly made it all the way back up the cobblestone path before the real downpour started. As soon as he heard that one big clap of thunder, he put his head down and broke into a full run, sprinting the last fifteen or twenty yards to the porch. Now he was out of breath and soaking wet, but not all that much moreso than he'd already been from trotting to the boathouse and back in the pre-storm drizzle. He counted himself lucky.

Seeing that someone had lit a fire, Rodney counted himself lucky again. He carried his dripping shoes across the room and set them on the stones in front of the hearth, then he pulled off his sodden jacket and hung it on the corner of the mantlepiece to dry.

He was still warming himself by the fire, and had just begun wondering where everyone else had got to, when Carson returned to the foyer from his exploration of the mansion's interior.

"What happened to you?" Carson asked. He thought Rodney looked a bit like an old cat that had just lost a fight with a goldfish bowl.

"There's a boat," Rodney replied, cutting directly to the chase. "In that little shed down by the docks. At least, I think so. There's a tarp over it, and the shed's locked, so I didn't get a good look."

"What good's a boat?" asked Carson.

"Umm... We could get off the island, maybe?" said Rodney. "You know, *survive the night* and all that?... fifty points sounds good enough to me."

"You can't take a boat out in this stuff," Carson said, meaning the rain.

"It's not gonna rain all night," Rodney countered. "Anyway, now we know it's there, so it's an option if we need it."

"You gotta lighten up, man," Carson said, chucking Rodney playfully on the shoulder. "Get in the spirit of things; roll with it. This place is really cool if you just look around a little. You should see the trophy room."

"Did you find something?"

"In the trophy room? Hell yes! There's a ton of dead animals, and axes and spears and stuff in there. It's pretty wild."

"I mean, anything like a *clue*... you know, what we're supposed to be doing for the final."

"I don't know... maybe? But we've got all night. I'm still just kind of poking around, but I'm loving this so far. The whole place is like an amusement park."

"More like a haunted house."

"You worry too much, man," Carson said, playfully bobbing and weaving around Rodney like a boxer. "Get with the zeitgeist. You said it yourself, it's a movie, right? So nobody survives a monster movie by running away. You gotta be tough and resourceful. Pull a John Wayne or something."

"John Wayne didn't do monster movies."

"OK, like Vincent Price then."

"Half the time, Vincent Price *was* the monster."

"So what? All I know is, the guy that runs away is one and done. But the *hero*..." Carson said with emphasis, "...the hero gets to come back for the sequels."

Rodney frowned, and let the conversation drop. He grabbed the fireplace poker and jabbed it at the coals a few times, before adding a couple more pieces of wood to the fire. Carson decided to give him some space, so he walked to the other side of the room, and took a long look at the grandfather clock. It was 8:56.

Eventually, Rodney had to admit to himself that he wasn't going to accomplish anything by standing in the foyer all night, and it might be better to play along with Carson's enthusiasm than to be left out of the loop entirely.

"So tell me about this trophy room then," he asked.

"Hah!... said Carson, who was feeling suddenly victorious. "Sure... but I'd hate to spoil the surprise. Better I just show you."

Rodney wasn't at all excited about the prospect of a surprise, whatever that might mean, but he'd already come this far. He nodded, reluctantly, and still in his stocking feet, followed Carson out of the foyer and down one of the adjoining hallways.

Not two minutes later, Shelby Oswald appeared on the balcony above, and made her way back down the curving staircase to the foyer, leaving the second floor to Liza, Meri, and Monroe. Shelby didn't doubt that the library was well worth investigating, and all things being equal she might have been perfectly content to help them explore it. But at the moment she had something else in mind.

She hadn't told the others where she was going, partly because she wanted to confirm her own guesses before involving the rest of the group, but mostly because she didn't want Monroe tagging along, either so he could be the first one to make fun of her if she was wrong, or so he could try and take all the credit later on, if she happened to be right. Monroe had been known to do that sort of thing.

But it was something Monroe had said that had given her the idea. He mentioned that the dumbwaiter might go all the way down to the wine cellar, and Shelby couldn't think of a more likely place to look for a hidden entrance to Professor Grimdeath's secret laboratory. Of course, she still couldn't be absolutely sure that there even *was* a secret laboratory. But her every instinct told her that there had to be one, and if there was, a wine cellar seemed to Shelby like it might be a prime spot to start looking.

She noticed the muddy shoes and the wet jacket by the fireplace, and puzzled briefly over whom they might belong to. She guessed that they must be Rodney's, though she had no idea why Rodney (or anyone else) would have gone outside in the driving rain.

She was still contemplating the jacket and the shoes when the foyer's grandfather clock began to strike. She jumped slightly at the unexpected sound, and turned around to look.

It was nine o'clock.

Shelby pursed her lips with impatience and frowned, but found she couldn't drag herself away from the foyer until the clock had fully chimed the hour. When it finally completed its ninth stroke she exhaled with relief, and set off down the long hallway from the foyer back to the dining room. From there she soon found her way to the kitchens, and was not entirely surprised to find that Dean was already there ahead of her, and rummaging through the cabinets. He heard the door from the hallway swing open, and looked back over his shoulder just long enough to confirm who it was.

"Shelby!" he said, returning to his explorations. "Having fun yet? I'm loving this kitchen, but I can't find *anything*..."

"What do you mean?" Shelby asked.

"Well, nothing's where it ought to be," Dean explained. "Everything's tucked away, but nothing's sensibly organized or convenient to get at. You'd think no one ever actually *cooks* here, like it's all just for show. It's maddening."

"You know..." Shelby said, "now that you mention it, the dining room was kind of the same way. I hadn't really thought about it much, but nothing in there really looked like it was meant to be used, either."

"AH!" said Dean, as he pulled a gleaming metal spatula out of one of the cabinet drawers. He turned to show off his discovery, and brandished it triumphantly, "Success at last. I've already got a skillet, and the range top works, but I still need a good mixing bowl. And a spoon...! I haven't even found the *silverware* yet; any guesses?"

He swept his arms out wide, gesturing to the enormous kitchen in the same way that a tour guide might have gestured to the vastness of the Rocky Mountains or the Grand Canyon. Shelby smiled. Like most people, she found it hard not to fall in love with Dean just a little bit, especially when he was in his element.

"You're the expert," she said, "I'll leave that to you. I'm looking for the basement, or the wine cellar. You wouldn't happen to know..."

"There." He replied firmly, cutting her off mid-question. He pointed the spatula dramatically toward a door that was tucked away between two cabinets in the far corner of the room. "That's the pantry; there's a staircase down to the cellar in there, and another little hallway too, but I don't know where it goes. I only took a peek."

"Thanks," said Shelby, as she crossed to the pantry door.

"Why the wine cellar?" Dean asked, curiously.

"Just a hunch," Shelby replied.

"Well if you find a cask of Amontillado down there, I don't want to know about it."

"Then I won't tell you," Shelby said, playfully. "Have fun with your cooking."

"Oh, I'm not cooking anything *right now*," Dean said, almost apologetically. "I'm just getting my ducks in a row for later, in case someone changes their mind. I know we've got more important things to do first. Have you found anything interesting yet?"

"Just the dining room," Shelby said, "Oh, and the library upstairs. I think some of the others are exploring that now. It's kind of huge."

"No surprises there," Dean replied, as he returned to rummaging through the cabinets. "Fun times for everybody."

Chapter 13:
...Seven to Go

While Shelby darted off in search of whatever she was searching for, the others decided to tackle the library. If the students' initial plan had been to scatter – so as to search as much of the house as possible in the least amount of time – the library flipped the script on that strategy. As large and as cluttered as it was, the room held no shortage of curiosities for Monroe, Liza, and Meri to puzzle over. Here, there was little danger that the three of them would be getting in each other's way any time soon.

Monroe started by scanning the titles in the bookcases along the outer walls. As it turned out, they were not as chaotically organized as they had first appeared. Each shelf seemed to hold to its own general theme or point of focus, though the books themselves varied wildly in their age, appearance, and general condition.

The first bookcase he came to held a broad cross-section of 19th-century fiction. The various works of Jane Austen, the Brontë sisters (including Anne), Dickens, Poe, Mary Shelley, Victor Hugo, Edward Bulwer-Lytton and many other authors both obscure and famous could be found lurking there, in copies ranging from dog-eared and irreplaceable first editions to unread modern paperbacks. Monroe looked over the shelf with a mixture of bemusement and disdain.

"Classic chick-lit..." he muttered to himself dismissively. "I had no idea Doctor G was a fan..."

As Monroe scanned the shelving, Meri wandered through the center of the room, glancing over the display cases and the reading tables. She found that one of the cases contained a Shakespearean first folio, while another held what appeared to be one of Leonardo Da Vinci's sketchbooks. She couldn't help wondering if these two literary treasures were really genuine, though they certainly appeared to be. She tried raising the glass top of the case that held the Da Vinci, to see if she could get a closer look, but it was securely locked and would not open.

Disappointed but not surprised, Meri moved on to the reading tables. The first one she came to was piled with what she took to be a selection of old children's books. There were several illustrated copies of *Mother Goose* and *The Brothers Grimm*, both in the original versions and in more modern editions. There were also some books that Meri did not immediately recognize, some of which were clearly not written in English. These included a hefty German tome *Gefahren der Nacht*, and a well worn leather-bound volume titled *La Bête du Gévaudan*, which Meri correctly assumed was written entirely in French. A copy of Joseph Jacobs' *English Fairy Tales* was just beside the largest stack of books; it had been left lying open to the familiar fable of *The Three Little Pigs*.

Elsewhere on the table, Meri found two books by Robert Louis Stevenson – *Dr. Jekyll and Mr. Hyde* and, curiously enough, *Travels with a Donkey in the Cévennes*. She puzzled briefly over the second of these two, as it did not seem to fit with what she took to be the table's general theme.

Though Monroe and Meri had chosen to devote their attention to the library's contents, Liza found herself most intrigued by its architecture. The room was large enough that it required a pair of central standing columns to support the full expanse of its vaulted ceiling. The space was generously illuminated by two hanging chandeliers, as well as from sconces along the outer walls. Floor lamps stood near some of the more comfortable chairs, while smaller lamps could be found on each of the reading tables.

Aside from the great double doors that led to the main hallway, and the carefully hidden servants' corridor from which they'd entered, the room had no other doors, or at least none that were readily obvious. Liza suspected however that considering the sheer size of the library, and given what they had already learned about the general layout of the mansion's upper story, there was likely to be another hidden portal somewhere in the room, and possibly even more than one.

During the day, the library's only natural light would have come from three deeply set alcoves along the rear wall, whose tall multi-paned windows spanned nearly the room's full height from the ceiling to the floor. The alcoves looked out over the mansion's formal gardens,

58

a large greenhouse and a rustic-looking gardener's shed, and then on to the rugged tangle of forest beyond.

Standing at one of those windows, Liza could see that the rain outside was no longer falling quite so heavily as it had been only a few minutes before. Some rumbles of thunder could still be heard, and the heavy sky still flickered overhead with occasional bursts of cloud lightning, but otherwise it seemed that the main storm had already passed, or at least had expended the bulk of its fury.

Situated beside the library's main entry, a grandfather clock – similar in design and appearance to the one that sat downstairs in the grand foyer – began to slowly chime the hour. It was now nine o'clock. The three students paused while the clock sounded, looking at each other somewhat uncomfortably. Only an hour had passed since their final exam had officially begun, and yet they each perceived the time slipping away from them somehow, and much more keenly than they had before.

No one said anything. None of them felt, for the moment at least, that they had anything of particular value to say. They returned to their respective searches, now helpfully equipped with a freshly renewed sense of unease.

Meri soon discovered that the books stacked on the second reading table all seemed to be about plants, in one way or another. She noted some popular modern titles, such as *The Botany of Desire*, alongside less-familiar volumes such as *Folk Remedies from Antiquity*, and *Horticultural Mysticism*.

She also spotted a well-worn copy of the notorious Voynich Manuscript – a cryptic codex of botanical and astrological material dating back to the early Renaissance, which had either been written in a complex alchemical code or in some bizarre unknown language. For several centuries it had famously defied all attempts at translation, and was now believed (at least by most reputable researchers) to be an extensive and elaborate fabrication, compiled by some inventive forger of the 15th century.

Near the center of the table was a large, folio-sized volume printed on heavy, slightly yellowed paper, and sturdily bound in dark leather. It was lying open to a hand-colored lithograph depicting a tall, leafy plant with a long central stem and a large cluster of dark purple flowers at the top. From the shape of the flowers, Meri guessed (incorrectly) that the plant in the picture might be some sort of wild orchid.

She closed the book and picked it up, only to discover that it was every bit as hefty as it looked. She couldn't help thinking how miserable it would be to have to lug a tome like that around campus in a backpack. She turned the book over to look at its spine, half-expecting the title to be something along the lines of "Intro to Botany" or "Wildflowers 101". But the actual title was far more interesting, and also more disturbing: *The Herbology of Poisons.* Meri was instantly alarmed.

"I think I've found something..." she said aloud, without looking up from the cover.

"So have I," said Liza, from the other side of the room.

Meri looked up from the book, and the two women stared at each other for a few seconds.

"What is it?" Meri asked.

"It'll wait," said Liza. "You first."

Meri looked down at the book again, and read the cover several more times, her mind racing with questions, and with the possible implications of this discovery.

"What about plants?" Meri said, looking up again. "Could the monster have something to do with plants, whatever it is? This was lying open here next to all these others. They're all related to botany somehow; this one's about plants and poisons."

"I don't know... Poison's more of a murder mystery thing, isn't it?" said Monroe, skeptically. "There's a whole bookcase of Agatha Christie around here somewhere, I remember seeing it. But the PowerPoint definitely said 'monster', and I can't see how poison's got anything to do with that."

"Well, I don't know..." Meri said hesitantly. "Some kind of plant monster...?"

"Audrey Two...!" Liza said playfully. Then she began to sing: "*Lit-tle shop; little shop of hor-rors...*" she stopped suddenly. "That's all I know," she said, almost bashfully. "I can't sing for shit... I bet Carson could probably do the whole musical for us, if we asked him."

"Let's not," said Monroe.

"I think plants must be important somehow," Meri insisted. She looked down at the book again, and read the cover aloud: "*The Herbology of Poisons*... this has got to be some sort of clue."

"I can't think of any other plant monsters," Liza said, more seriously. "Venus fly traps, but that's about it. Maybe it's something else about plants... like a transformation, or garlic for vampires or something."

"I hate to break it to you," said Monroe, "but garlic isn't poisonous."

"We're brainstorming here," Liza said, giving Monroe a nasty look.

"Liza, what did *you* find?" Meri asked, hoping to change the subject, and maybe short-circuit a brewing argument before it reached full bloom. She wanted to keep things moving along in a positive light, and had no reservations about mixing her metaphors if she had to. Shaken, not stirred.

Lizabel bit her lip and looked at the floor for a minute, containing her temper. She wasn't eager to let Monroe off the hook for being his usual self, but she also knew that a full-scale argument wasn't going to accomplish anything. She relented.

"I found another door," she finally said, somewhat reluctantly. She looked up at Monroe and glared at him for a moment longer, before turning to Meri. "It's right here," she added, pointing over her left shoulder at the bookcase behind her. "There's a hidden latch underneath the third shelf."

Chapter 14:
Pistols and Pantries

Rodney wasn't nearly so excited by the trophy room as Carson had been. Rodney liked animals, and seeing so many dead ones – including some that were certainly endangered or even already extinct – made him uncomfortable. He reminded himself that most of the trophies were probably a hundred years old or more, and that many of them (such as the unicorn) were almost certainly fakes. The thought made him feel a little better.

But what Rodney was most interested in were the antique weapons, and his interest was purely a practical one. It seemed logical to him that if they were going to have to kill some sort of as-yet-unidentified monster, they were going to need something to kill it *with*, regardless of whether it was real or only hypothetical for the sake of their exam. Or barring that, maybe they could make good use of a sturdy axe or a spear in some other way. Rodney had not given up on his original plan of simply escaping the island by boat, and he wasn't at all above the idea of smashing or prying open that little padlock on the boathouse door.

Or shooting it...

"Are these real, do you think?" Rodney asked, pointing to the matched dueling pistols in the display case.

"I don't know, maybe," Carson said. "Why?"

"If there's gonna be a monster, don't you think a gun or two might come in handy?" Rodney pointed out. "And look, there's one for both of us."

Rodney tried raising the case's glass top, and was surprised to find that it was unlocked. It lifted easily, and once it was fully open a hinged peg on the underside dropped down to conveniently hold it in place.

"Nice," said Carson.

The dueling pistols were indeed very nice. Their grips were made of polished ebony, and their dark octagonal barrels were tastefully ornamented with a fine tracery of gold inlay. Lovingly crafted, the pair provided a most elegant means by which two sophisticated and well-bred gentlemen might murder each other. Nestled together on the green velvet fabric of their display case, they presented themselves as a triumphant irony of early 19th century civilized culture.

———————————

Liza tripped the hidden catch she'd found, but the bookcase did not move. She tried pulling it away from the wall and it grudgingly shifted, but only a tiny bit. The gap she'd made was not nearly wide enough for her to squeeze through, and she could not budge the bookcase another inch, at least not by herself. Peering through the narrow opening, she could see nothing at all; the empty space beyond was forbiddingly dark.

Meri and Monroe came to help, and the three of them together were able to drag the bookcase out a little bit further, though it wasn't easy. The rusted iron hinges that had held it in place groaned as they slowly relented. Now there was a gap of several inches between the bookcase and the wall: still a tight squeeze for Liza or Meri at best, and likely an impossible fit for Monroe.

"It's dragging on the carpet," Meri said. "It's pretty well stuck."

"Let's unload the books," Monroe suggested. "That might help."

They couldn't reach the topmost shelves, not without a step-ladder, but they didn't need to. Once they'd removed most of the books from the lower part of the case, it swung on its hinges a little more easily, and they were finally able to pull it the rest of the way open.

The passageway behind was still very dark. There was no carpet, the hardwood flooring was made of black walnut, and the walls were paneled with some other sort of equally somber and unreflective wood. There did not appear to be any lighting fixtures at all, electric or otherwise; not overhead, nor even along the walls. For whatever reason, it seemed that this little corridor was deliberately intended to be left totally dark.

With what little light spilled in from the library, the three students could see that the passageway ran straight for only a few steps before making a sharp left turn back toward the front of the house. Beyond that ninety-degree corner they could see nothing at all; the darkness was nearly complete. They stood together at that corner and gazed into the void for some time.

"Who's got a flashlight?" said Meri, unhappily.

"I would have to say this qualifies as seriously creepy," Liza agreed.

Monroe snapped his fingers sharply. He'd suddenly remembered something.

"I think..." he said cryptically, "I know where to find some candles."

Shelby was standing in the pantry and feeling very excited. There wasn't anything particularly exciting about the pantry; but her excitement had little to do with the pantry itself. Her excitement was rooted in anticipation; anticipation of what might lie *beyond* the pantry. She felt herself standing at the very cusp of possibility.

So it is with all of us perhaps, at certain moments in our lives. We find ourselves in familiar and ordinary circumstances, surrounded by ordinary things, and yet we are filled with a sense of something greater, something just beyond our reach, beyond our sight. Something transformative, perhaps. Something indescribable. Something wonderful. We sense that we are standing at a nexus of possibility and potential, and if only the dice will fall in our favor just this once, everything might suddenly change.

Such moments are rare, and to be treasured, for they do not last, and never turn out entirely as we might have hoped or imagined. That uncertainty lies at the core of their allure.

For Shelby, this was just such a moment.

The pantry was illuminated by a glass-domed electric fixture mounted to the ceiling. The light was sufficient for her to see the entire room and its contents clearly, but by no means was it bright or cheerful. The pantry walls were lined with ordinary wooden storage shelves. Some of them held cans or jars or sacks or boxes of various foodstuffs and non-perishables, but most were empty. Shelby was also pleased to see the dumbwaiter. It was exactly where she'd expected it to be, just to her left as she came through the door, which confirmed that her general sense of the mansion's floorplan was at least somewhat accurate.

Opposite the door through which she'd entered, she spied the little hallway that Dean had mentioned. It seemed to run straight ahead, on toward the front of the mansion. Shelby suspected that it was another servants' corridor similar to the one that she and the others had found in the walk-in closet upstairs. She wondered briefly where the other end of that passageway might emerge, but that was a question that would have to wait for later. For the moment, Shelby's interests lay elsewhere. Her only real concern was the staircase on the other side of the room. A little wooden staircase going down.

Rodney and Carson each lifted one of the pistols, and found them to be surprisingly heavy. Carson had handled stage pistols on several occasions, but had little experience with real firearms. Rodney, on the other hand, had never in his life fired any sort of gun at all.

"I'm pretty sure these are real," said Rodney, hopefully. Carson nodded in tentative agreement.

"They're really cool," he said. "But I don't know how to load a gun like this; do you?"

"I think they might be already loaded," Rodney guessed, trying awkwardly to look down the barrel of his, without actually pointing it at himself. "I think that was customary for dueling pistols."

"In a display case, though?" said Carson, skeptically. "I dunno... that seems like a reach."

"I bet Monroe would know..." Rodney replied. "This is his kind of thing. Didn't he go to a military academy or something?"

"I have no idea," Carson replied.

Eventually, the two of them agreed that some sort of test firing was in order. There were two guns, after all, and it stood to reason that they would either both be loaded or both be empty; and trying to shoot something with one of them would (theoretically, at least) confirm the question for both. If the gun didn't fire, they'd know they needed to load it, while if it did fire, they'd still have one working pistol in hand if need be.

And Rodney, of course, already had a suitable test target in mind.

Carson wasn't at all excited by the prospect of wandering out into the darkness and the rain, but he had to admit that the worst of the storm seemed to have already passed, and he hadn't forgotten that the path to the docks was at least partially illuminated.

Carson was, however, *very* excited by the idea of shooting the padlock off of the boathouse door. It seemed to him so quintessentially heroic... it was the sort of thing he could easily picture Steve McQueen, or Humphrey Bogart, or Samuel L. Jackson, or any number of his other heroes doing in a desperate spot, and without a moment's hesitation.

But more importantly, Carson knew that in a typical buddy picture *both* the main characters tended to survive. He'd begun to suspect that he and Rodney were in the early stages of forming just that sort of relationship, and if nurturing that meant taking a long and useless walk back down the hill to the boat docks, well so be it. Anything that upped Carson's chances to cast himself in the hero's role seemed like a sound investment in his book.

And what's more, even in movies where both the buddies *didn't* survive, it was almost always the sidekick who bought the farm, and not the hero. That seemed like an insurance policy worth having. In Carson's deeply theatrical mind, a guy like Rodney had all the makings of a classically expendable supporting character.

Perfect.

Chapter 15:
Different Doorways

Carson and Rodney made their way carefully down the cobblestone path to the boat dock. They tucked the dueling pistols underneath their jackets, in an effort to keep them dry. But the rain had let up considerably from what it had been only a few minutes before, and was now once again little more than a fine drizzle of mist in the air.

They reached the boathouse without incident, and Carson peered through the little four-paned window at the tarp-covered lump inside.

"Might be a boat..." he said. "I can't tell for sure."

"The doors are over here," said Rodney, walking around to the unlit side of the building. He tugged briefly at the padlock, but it was securely latched. He took a deep breath and looked at Carson.

"Well," he said hesitantly, "I guess this is it. You or me?"

"This was all your idea," Carson said. "Go for it."

Rodney leveled his pistol at the lock, and tried pulling the hammer back with his thumb, but the spring was too strong for him, and he couldn't do it cleanly. Embarrassed, he reached up and cocked the gun with his left hand. Carson stifled a grin.

"OK... here goes," Rodney said, gritting his teeth and holding his left arm up to shield his eyes. Carson took a couple of steps backwards.

Rodney pulled the trigger, and the gun went off like a thunderclap. The noise of it was almost deafening; much louder than either he or Carson had expected. Rodney's wrist bent back with the recoil, and the smoking stench of black powder filled the air.

"Son of a bitch!" said Rodney.

"I guess it *was* loaded." said Carson.

"You noticed that, did you?"

"That was loud. Did it work?"

Rodney looked down at the lock, but it was no longer there. It had been blown clean away.

"Yes!" he said. "It's open!"

With the lock gone, the doors pulled open easily, and when they looked inside the two young men found that there was indeed a boat there. It was a small motorboat, already mounted on a light double-wheeled trailer, and ready to be towed down the highway behind someone's pickup truck.

Carson smiled and nodded, while Rodney felt like he'd just won the lottery.

Monroe hadn't said where he was going, but Liza and Meri both guessed that he was headed back to the grand foyer. They hadn't forgotten that there had been some candles there, mounted along the interior walls. In any event, neither of them had any intention of sitting on their hands waiting for Monroe to return.

They first tried moving one of the library's floor lamps into the unlit corridor, but its cord was too short to reach all the way from the nearest outlet. They succeeded in getting a little more light into the entryway, and pushed the darkness back by another couple of yards, but it wasn't nearly enough.

Like any good technician, Meri had a Swiss army knife in the pocket of her jeans, and she was sorely tempted to cut the cord off of one of the other lamps. She suspected that if she spliced the wires together, she could probably make a workable extension. But she was hesitant to vandalize any of the library's antique furnishings if she could help it, and Liza pointed out that even if they could get one of the electric lamps further inside, it might still not be enough to throw light all the way to the far end of that long shadowy hall.

Frustrated but undaunted, the two women continued to search for a solution, and eventually struck gold. In the servants' corridor on the opposite side of the room, Meri found a small box of votive candles and a tin filled with kitchen matches tucked away on a shelf near the dumbwaiter. She guessed that they had been put there for emergency use, in the event of a power outage.

They each set one of the little candles inside of a whiskey tumbler, and voila! They were now equipped with a pair of functional – if somewhat less than convenient – makeshift lanterns.

As she descended the basement stairs, Shelby discovered that the wine cellar was not illuminated even as well as the pantry had been. The only light came from a single, uncovered bulb, overhead in the center of the room. There was a dry, musty smell of old bricks and unfinished wood.

Along the walls she could see racks of wine bottles, cradled on their sides. She picked one of the bottles up at random, and tried to read its label, but it was difficult to see clearly in the dim light. She brushed the dust off, carried it to the center of the room, and held it up to the light for a closer look. The label was slightly faded, and read "L'Abbaye Bessèges – 1873."

She carefully returned the bottle to where she had found it, then slowly made her way around the perimeter of the room, hoping to find some secret latch or lever that might reveal a hidden door such as they'd found in the upstairs closet. To her surprise however, she found not a door, but an open archway in the corner of the room. In the poor light, she simply hadn't noticed it before.

She stepped through and found herself in a chamber almost identical to the one she'd just come from. Apparently Professor Grimdeath was more of a wine aficionado than she'd guessed. This second portion of the cellar was, if anything, even more dingy and dimly lit than the first. But more significant to Shelby than the racks of dust-covered bottles was a faint light on the far wall, at about shoulder height. She walked over to it.

It was a flat metal panel with a square white button at its center, directly beside a large metal door. The door itself was smooth and featureless, and framed by some sort of sturdy resin enclosure. The whole apparatus looked decidedly out of place. It was entirely unlike anything else she'd seen in the mansion so far, and was completely out of character for the rustic wine cellar. To Shelby, it looked very much like an airlock out of a modern science fiction movie.

She could feel her heart racing. Her hand trembled only slightly as she reached out and pressed the glowing white button. She heard a faint *whoosh* of air, as the pressure seals at the edges released. Then the metal door slid briskly aside, and Shelby Oswald stepped through the opening into Doctor Grimdeath's hidden laboratory.

Chapter 16:
Where Darkness Dwells

Meri and Liza made their way very cautiously down the dark hidden corridor. Their candles provided scarcely enough light for them to see the wooden flooring beneath their feet and the walls to either side, but looking ahead they could still see nothing at all. The shadows before them seemed almost to devour the fluttering candlelight.

They pressed forward, further into the gloom, with Liza walking a few feet ahead. Meri looked back over her shoulder, and saw the hallway's right-angle corner shining pale behind her. It seemed a hundred yards away, though they had only walked perhaps a half-dozen paces. She dragged her eyes forward again, and with a few quick steps caught up to Liza, who was still making her way slowly down the passage.

After what seemed like an eternity, though it could not have been more than a minute or two at the most, Liza spotted something in the darkness ahead. At first she could not tell what it was; she could see only the vaguest hint of a shape, a tiny defect in the otherwise perfect darkness. But as she drew closer it became more distinct, as if the shadows around her were somehow weaving themselves into a solid form.

What she had first seen was the bottom end of a staircase handrail. The staircase itself soon came into view: a tightly circling spiral going up. Liza stopped at the foot of the bottom stair and turned back to Meri. Their eyes met, and the two young women looked at each other for a long moment.

"Do you hear it?" Meri asked, very quietly.

"Hear what?"

"Listen..."

Liza closed her eyes and listened as hard as she could, but she heard nothing at all, only their own breathing and the quiet murmur of the wind outside. Then she realized that it wasn't the wind. It was more like a distant flute, playing some sort of wandering and tuneless melody in a very low register. She opened her eyes and looked up at her companion.

"Background music..." Meri whispered.

"I don't know if that's good or bad," Liza replied.

They listened for a few moments longer, but there was nothing left to be said. They'd come this far, and their only remaining choice was to either go back or go up. They each took a deep breath, and slowly began to climb.

Though the hallway had seemed endless, this little spiral staircase did not. It climbed steeply for a total of only eighteen steps – Meri counted them – before it emerged at an open archway facing into a small octagonal room. There were windows in three of the walls, but they provided no illumination. Outside, the sky was pitch dark, and a light rain was still falling, but even had there been full moonlight it would not have mattered; all three of the windows were fully shrouded with heavy black curtains.

Although neither of them noticed it immediately, the music had stopped.

"What sort of place is *this*...?" Liza whispered, more to herself than to her companion.

"We're at the top of the turret," Meri said, in equally hushed tones. "I think we must be."

Though their candles offered no better light than before, their eyes had adjusted somewhat to the darkness, and now that there was something other than an empty hallway for them to look at, Liza and Meri found that they could see well enough to at least get a general sense of the room.

At the center of the octagon was a low, rectangular stone table. It was not more than three feet long, with the surface of its top only slightly higher than Lizabel's knee. At each of the room's eight corners stood a short stone pillar, cylindrical in shape, holding a large half-burned candle. The candles were unlit. Lying on the floor beside the stone table, and scattered elsewhere throughout the room, were several neatly bundled clumps of wildflowers.

Meri's heart sank all the way to her shoes.

"Aww... no!..." She moaned, looking around the room, despondently.

"What is it?" asked Liza.

"It's not fair...!" Meri continued, miserably. "Why couldn't it have been a killer robot? I could have *rocked* a killer robot! But this is a *demon summoning*, right? What am I supposed to do with a demon?! I mean this stuff might be right up your alley, but this is so far out of my zone... Damnit...! I'm gonna flunk this *so bad*.... oh god damn it, it just isn't fair." She dropped her head and stood sulking in the archway.

Liza stepped further into the room and took a careful look at her surroundings with a practiced and critical eye. She could understand Meri's disappointment. If the monster *had* turned out to be a killer robot, or some sort of murderous alien slime creature from outer space or any of a dozen other high-tech perils, she would probably have felt just as hopeless as Meri was feeling now.

And Meri was right about something else as well... this *was* Liza's specialty. She probably knew more about arcane rituals and demonology than anyone else in the group. She suddenly felt the added weight of that responsibility on her shoulders. The others needed her. She had to get this right. She had to think.

"I don't think this was a summoning," Liza said, after a few moments. "The candles are wrong. There should be five of them, or six maybe, but not eight. And there's no circle marked out for the creature to emerge from; no gateway." She looked down at the stone table, or the altar if that's what it was. Her confidence was growing as she spoke. "And there's no runes of power, either... none that I can see. There's nothing here to bind a summoned creature in place, or control it. Without something like that, a demon might just tear the summoner to shreds, then go back to the netherworld... Doctor G wouldn't be that careless... No, I think this has to be something else..."

"Then what is it?" Meri asked.

"I don't know yet," Liza replied. "Help me look, but try not to touch anything."

The two women carefully searched the room, and soon found some curious details that they hadn't noticed before.

"You know... I think whatever happened here happened more than once," Meri speculated. "Lots of times, I'd guess."

"Why do you say that?" Liza asked.

"Look at all the wax that's dripped off these candles," Meri said. "They've burned way down. But if you burn a fat candle like this all at once, it gets lopsided, and collapses on itself, or the wick melts out to one side. But these have melted evenly all the way down. That probably means they were used lots of times, but never for very long at once. Maybe an hour or so, maybe even less than that."

"That would fit," said Liza. "Look at this table. There's a patch of soot near the center, and some loose strands of grey hair as well. I think some of them have been burned."

"What does it all mean?"

"It's not a demon summoning," Liza said. "I'm sure of that much; this set-up couldn't even summon a pokémon. But I don't know what else it might have been for. Maybe a purification rite of some sort, or a warding ritual perhaps. Not to bring something here, but rather trying to *keep something away*..."

"Creature from the Black Lagoon?" Meri suggested, more than half-seriously. "Maybe something that was already living on the island?"

"What are all these flowers?" Liza said. "That's what puzzles me most."

Meri hadn't really paid any notice to the clumps of weeds before, but now she looked at them a little more closely.

"You know what..." she said hesitantly, "I think these were in that book... the one that was lying open in the library."

"Now *that's* interesting," Liza said. "Should we take some back with us just to make sure?"

"And speaking of the library," said Meri, looking strangely puzzled, "where the hell is Monroe?"

Chapter 17:
About the Candles

Monroe was taking his sweet time.

He'd left Liza and Meri in the library, and gone off to fetch some candles, but he was in no hurry about it. As far as he knew, most of the mansion's second floor still hadn't been properly investigated, and all things being equal Monroe preferred to do his own searching, rather than simply following up on other people's hunches. He still intended to bring some candles back to the library – all in due time – but first he wanted to do a little more exploring on his own, without anyone else's interference. He was sure the girls could find plenty of ways to keep themselves busy in the meantime; and after all, that new secret passageway wasn't going anywhere. It could wait.

As he made his way along the winding upstairs hall, he stopped to try each door he came to. The first one he passed was a tiny bathroom, barely large enough for an ordinary stool and a sink. The second was a bedroom much like the one he'd seen before, though smaller, and apparently with no closet or windows. Seeing nothing there that grabbed his interest, he moved on. But with the third door he finally found something that seemed to merit a closer look.

He pushed the door open and found himself in what appeared to be a poorly organized study or private office. There was a cluttered roll-top writing desk set against the far wall, with an oak-veneer filing cabinet standing opposite. An old bentwood office chair – complete with wooden casters and an upholstered fabric seat cushion – had been pulled away from the desk, and left facing out at an odd angle, as if its occupant had never bothered to put it back into place. There were no other doors in the room, though deeply set into the far wall, high above the cabinet and the desk, were a pair of small clerestory windows.

Monroe was immediately intrigued, though he more than half-suspected that this little office, like so much else in the house, was only for show, and not a place where any of the doctor's real work was done.

For one thing there was no computer, only old envelopes and calendars, appointment books and a few odd notes hastily scribbled onto random scraps of paper. Monroe couldn't imagine that any useful work could come from so much chaos. In his mind, genius was a product of discipline.

But by the same token, given its obviously contrived nature, this little office seemed very much like the sort of place where Doctor G might have planted an important clue. Monroe leaned his pool cue against the wall, cracked his knuckles, and decided to investigate the room a little bit further.

He rummaged briefly through the papers on the desk, but nothing leapt out at him as being obviously important. The desktop calendar was more than five years out of date, and most of the notes seemed to relate to minor details of a trip that the professor had taken through Europe at around that same time.

Monroe pulled open the top drawer of the filing cabinet, and found several dozen sheafs of hand-written notes, all neatly tucked into file folders with cryptic labels such as *Crone Outside of Belgrade* or *Hermit Near Strasbourg*. Monroe guessed that these were transcriptions of interviews the professor had held with villagers in various locales during his trip, but he could not determine what exactly the professor had been researching. Most of the transcripts were written in languages which Monroe could not hope to read, though he would occasionally spot an intriguing word or two of English scribbled in the margins with red ink: *Witchcraft... Fire... Transformation... Uprising... Affliction... Death....*

Monroe pushed the file cabinet closed again, and pondered what it all might mean. Images of angry peasants marching with pitchforks and torches in hand flashed through his mind, and he smiled at the cliché. But he also knew that clichés were often deeply rooted in truth.

Carson took the rope lead from the prow of the speedboat and tied it off to one of the support posts along the side of the wooden pier.

He and Rodney had muscled the little boat, trailer and all, out the front of the shed, and down to the water's edge. Fortunately the shoreline around that little cove was fairly flat and even, and covered in pebbles and small stones. So despite the rain it was not particularly sloppy or muddy.

Even so, manhandling the boat and trailer had been a lot of work, requiring ample cursing and multiple stops to rest and rethink their approach. But considering the fact that it was dark and raining, and that neither of them really knew what the hell they were doing, they had managed reasonably well: they'd eventually gotten the boat safely into the water without any significant damage, either to it or to themselves.

The speedboat had only two seats: a pair of small swiveling chairs mounted on posts and facing the control console. There was, however an open area behind those chairs where two or three more people might be able to squeeze themselves in – somewhat uncomfortably perhaps – and ride in relative safety, so long as they remained sitting on the flat decking of the boat's fiberglass floor.

The darkness made it difficult for Rodney and Carson to search the shed completely, but they did manage to locate four adult-sized foam-rubber life vests, and a gigantic inflatable novelty pool float in the shape of the Loch Ness Monster. The float had apparently never been used, as it was still sealed in its original packaging. They stowed these various flotation devices on the floor of the boat, then covered it over again with the tarpaulin. The rain had largely stopped, but they thought it best to keep the boat covered, just in case.

It is perhaps worth mentioning that they did *not* go to the trouble of fully inflating Nessie; they were much too out of breath to even make the attempt.

Rodney was all for setting sail immediately, but he wasn't surprised when Carson shot the idea down, and he didn't push the issue. He already felt much better, just knowing that the boat was ready for a quick getaway if the need arose. Leaning against the wall of the shed, he took a quick sip from his water bottle. He winced slightly as he swallowed, then coughed a few times.

"What have you got in that thing?" Carson asked, only half joking. "Tequila?"

"Gatorade," Rodney replied truthfully. "Fruit punch flavor, but I don't drink it straight. I cut it a little with vodka – takes the edge off."

Having exhausted his curiosity in the little office, Monroe continued down the hallway until he reached the balcony above the grand foyer. Standing at the rail and looking down, he found himself immensely puzzled, and trying to make sense of what he was seeing. The room certainly hadn't looked like this when he'd come through less than an hour before. There was a large puddle of water on the floor just inside the entryway, and someone had tracked mud all across the Persian rug. The front doors were standing wide open, and a cold wind was blowing in from outside.

"What a *mess...*" he said to himself.

And for some reason there was music playing as well. Monroe looked around at the ceiling and the walls, but there were no loudspeakers that he could see. He wondered where the music was coming from, but mostly he wondered why it had started playing *now*. There hadn't been music in the foyer when he'd come through before. There might have been something during the PowerPoint, when they all first arrived, but that was quiet and understated... nothing like the brooding orchestral piece that was playing now.

To be perfectly honest, Monroe thought the music was a little over the top. He wasn't a big fan of Doctor G's penchant for melodrama, but there it was. He wondered if there was some sort of computer program controlling when and where the music played. He assumed there must be... maybe something like a b-movie hack of Pandora or Spotify.

Monroe made his way down the stairs to the main floor. He stepped carefully around the puddle of water and went to the open entryway. Looking up and down the front porch, he couldn't see anyone anywhere around, but there were more muddy footprints on the porch outside, as well as those inside the door... in fact there was mud smeared on the floor almost everywhere. It seemed that more than one person with muddy feet had come that way.

Looking at the footprints more closely, Monroe realized that someone or other must have been barefoot. Now *this* was a puzzle. Monroe couldn't imagine why anyone would have gone out in the pouring rain in the first place, but why on Earth would anyone have been *barefoot*, and why would they have left the front door standing wide open when they came back inside? It was all a complete mystery to him.

He pulled the door closed, and looked around the room, trying to somehow make sense of it all. A fire was still burning in the fireplace; the suit of armor and the marble statue were just as they'd been before. Nothing seemed to have been moved. The same PowerPoint slide was showing on the video screen. The hands of the grandfather clock now marked the time as 9:38.

He noticed that one of the candles along the wall had been lit. That seemed odd to him. He was sure none of the candles had been burning before. He wondered briefly why someone would have lit only one candle. But seeing it reminded him of why he was there in the first place. It was probably high time for him to get back to the library – the girls were waiting for him after all, and by now they would almost certainly be wondering where he was.

He set his pool cue down against the fireplace, and was just reaching for one of the unlit candles when he heard a familiar clattering noise, slightly above the pulse of the music. The sound was so unexpected that it took Monroe a moment to realize that what he was hearing was the rattle of billiard balls, coming from just down one of the interior hallways. Apparently someone else had found the pool table, and was having a game. Not any sort of *regulation* game, of course: when Monroe had searched the room before he hadn't even been able to find the cue ball.

Intrigued, he stepped down the hallway to the billiard room. He found the door standing open, but the room appeared to be empty; there was no one there. He stepped inside and saw that the balls on the table were no longer neatly racked together, and there only seemed to be seven of them now. But who had been playing the game?

It was then that two hands with long curling fingers wrapped themselves tightly around his throat from behind, and began to squeeze. Monroe was thrown forward, face-down onto the felt of the pool table, then jerked backwards again with impossible strength, as jagged claws tore at his flesh. Too late he understood that someone – some *thing* – had been waiting for him behind the door, and that the clatter of the billiard balls had been meant only to lure him in. Monroe's final moments were a blur of astonishment and self-reproach, until darkness consumed him.

The music fell silent again.

A few moments later, only six balls remained, scattered atop the pool table. Along the inner wall of the grand foyer, two candles now were burning.

Chapter 18:
Flowers and Flatware

Shelby was disappointed.

She'd been right: She'd found a laboratory, and she'd found it right where she'd guessed it would be.

But she'd also been wrong: This lab wasn't all that secret, and it wasn't at all the sort of laboratory she'd hoped for, or expected to find. She'd expected to find something akin to Frankenstein's workshop from the old Boris Karloff movies, complete with grey stone walls covered in dials and gauges and electrical transformers, with heavy switches activating arcing circuits and other strange devices and machinery. Or barring that, something astonishingly high-tech, with flat-panel displays and gleaming white robotic components everywhere.

But this looked more like an ordinary chemistry lab; one that might not seem out of place on any college campus. It was not filled with mysterious antique equipment, but with traditional glassware, standard work benches covered with flasks and pipettes and Bunsen burners; all modern, or perhaps even a few decades out of date. The whole lab seemed to be entirely ordinary. She almost felt like she was back in high school.

It was a serious let-down, there was no way around it.

She walked down the little flight of metal stairs from the entry landing to the lab's main work floor. She wondered briefly why the lab itself had been built below the level of the entry. The reason was actually quite simple and practical. In the event of an accident or chemical spill, there would be less chance of any contaminants seeping out into the rest of the basement. And in a serious emergency, the entire floor could be flooded with water, or with a neutralizing foam, or with whatever other chemical counteragent might be required.

Shelby knew her way around a chemistry lab. Her major was Pre-Med, and she had once planned to become a surgical oncologist. She was no longer certain that was a career path she wanted to follow, but that didn't matter right now. She looked around at all the conventional laboratory glassware and her shoulders sagged. How could any sort of monster be fabricated *here*, she wondered. There didn't even seem to be a DNA sequencer, or anything more sophisticated than a centrifuge or a refractory spectrometer.

Shelby bit her lip, and tried to set her disappointment aside. "I'm missing something here..." she told herself. "There has to be a reason for all of this... what would it all be used for?"

She looked more closely at the way the various components had been arranged. She couldn't be certain, but her best guess was that most of the lab seemed to be set up for distillation processes of one type or another, but Shelby couldn't imagine that all this equipment would be necessary for anything so simple as making wine or beer... and why would the laboratory door need an airtight seal?

Then she noticed a smallish cardboard box sitting on one of the lab benches. It was nearly full with little purple wildflowers. Shelby thought they looked very much like the ones she'd seen on the dining room table, but she didn't know what sort of flower they were.

Was Doctor G distilling the fragrance of those flowers for some sort of experimental perfume?...

She wondered.

"Dean...!" she suddenly exclaimed, slapping herself on the forehead. "Dean's an Organic Chemistry major; *he'll* know what all this is for."

With her excitement instantly rekindled, Shelby rushed back through the darkness of the wine cellar and up the wooden stairs toward the pantry and the kitchens.

After what felt like an hour of searching, Dean had located most of the kitchen gadgets and utensils that he was looking for. He still hadn't found any silverware, however, and that bothered him. He decided to search the adjoining rooms, to see what else he could turn up.

Just off the kitchen, on the far side from the pantry, there was a short and narrow hallway that led to two unimpressive little rooms. The first of these appeared to be a dining room, though it was much smaller and less elegant than the formal dining room that Shelby had explored earlier in the evening. There were six simple wooden chairs, tightly clustered around a very plain – though sturdy – pinewood table. An equally rustic cabinet was against the opposite wall.

Dean guessed that the room was a *servants' mess* – not a showplace intended for the master of the house or his guests, but an out-of-the-way spot where the housekeeping staff and the other hired hands could sit down and eat, without disturbing anyone important.

He found it almost comical that there even was such a room here. Though the mansion was (for the most part) a faithful reproduction of the Victorian Gothic style, having a servants' dining room seemed like an ironic absurdity, given that Doctor Grimdeath did not appear to have any actual servants.

Dean went to the cabinet and pulled open the top drawer, and was pleasantly surprised to finally find some forks and knives, though the flatware in the drawer was no more impressive than anything else in the room. It was all cheap dime-store quality stuff, certainly not real silver, and not even consistent in its design. It looked as if the unwanted remnants of half a dozen mismatched sets had been unceremoniously dumped together into the drawer.

"Good enough for the help..." he said, picking up an old fork with bent tines, and looking it over ruefully. "True to the spirit of the age, I guess. But I do have to wonder where he's hidden all the good silver." Seeing nothing else of interest in the servants' mess, Dean decided to move on.

The other room along the little hallway had an outside door, and also a window facing out to the greenhouse and the gardens. Dean guessed it was a mud room, where the gardeners or other outside help could take off their muddy boots, and change clothes if need be, before going anywhere else inside the house. There was a large washbasin with running water, a pair of small benches, and some wooden pegs along the wall for coats and hats. At the far end of the room there was a little staircase; it mounted up to a small landing before doubling back on itself and continuing to the upper story. Like everything else in this part of the house, Dean suspected that the staircase was intended only for the servants, to provide them with a route to the upper floor without using the stairs in the grand foyer. It was a conceit of the age that 'the help' should be kept out of sight whenever possible.

Peering out the window, Dean could see that the rain had let up considerably. There was no more than a light mist falling now, though the wind was still blowing some droplets from the roof of the house and the branches of the trees.

Dean was tempted to explore the little staircase to the second floor, but he thought he'd heard a door opening somewhere behind him, and wondered if Shelby had found whatever she'd been looking for in the wine cellar. In any event, he was tired of rummaging around all by himself, so he decided to head back. He knew it was probably high time he started taking this final exam business more seriously, and maybe he could ease himself into it by teaming up with Shelby for a bit.

With that thought in mind, he headed back to the kitchen.

Meri and Liza made their way back down the unlit corridor. As soon as they reached the library, Meri dropped the bundle of flowers she'd been carrying onto the nearest table and shuddered.

"Nnnng..." she said, grimacing uncomfortably. "My fingers are tingling."

"Seriously?..." Liza asked. "Maybe we should be more careful with these. They might be more dangerous than they look."

The two women walked across the library to the servants' corridor, and washed their hands in the sink. Liza hadn't carried any of the flowers back with her, though she'd picked up one of the clumps briefly back in the octagonal room, and she wasn't inclined to take any chances.

"Are you ok?"

"I think so," said Meri, flexing her fingers. "The pins and needles are gone... but it felt like my hand was asleep, like I'd hit my funny bone or something."

They returned to the library, and wrapped the purple flowers in a tea towel so they wouldn't have to touch them. Then they started searching through *The Herbology of Poisons*, but it took them quite some time to find the picture Meri had seen earlier. Meri scolded herself for not having bookmarked the page before closing the book, but she'd been so eager to see the book's title, she hadn't considered that the page it was open to might be just as important.

There were dozens of images in the book, and the two curious students couldn't help stopping to read some of the more interesting descriptions. Many of the plants listed were already familiar to them as poisons, such as belladonna and hemlock. But there were others that they'd never heard of before, and a few that came as total surprises. Neither of them had known, for instance, that raw lima beans were potentially toxic.

They had just finished reading the entry for mandrake root, when they finally came to the page they were looking for. Even Liza, who hadn't seen the image before, instantly recognized the purple flowers. When she read the name, she gasped audibly.

"Son of a bitch..." she whispered.

"*Monk's hood*..." said Meri, reading the heading aloud. "I've never heard of it."

"Yes you have," said Liza, "but you know it by a different name."

"So what is it?"

"Monk's hood is another name for *wolfsbane*..." Liza replied. "That's what all those purple flowers are... they're wolfsbane."

Meri looked up at Liza as the realization slowly sank in. If the flowers were wolfsbane, then that meant the monster had to be a werewolf.

And if they were right, and the monster really *was* a werewolf, then she and Liza had just earned twenty-five points each.

Score. Bonding moment. Fist bump. High five.

Chapter 19:
A Wolf at the Door

As Shelby rushed through the shadows of the wine cellar on her way back to the kitchens, she felt so filled with excitement that she hardly noticed the music.

It was so perfectly in tune with her mood: bursting with energy – a snare drum and a top hat cymbal lightly pattering a quick staccato rhythm as a horn section provided the dramatic melody and a piano filled the gaps with sharply bursting, slightly discordant arpeggios. It was like the theme music for some short-lived 1970s television detective drama, written to be played over the opening credits while the hero raced his Gran Torino with the custom paint job through a gritty urban landscape in pursuit of drug dealers, fleeing in their dark green Cadillac Eldorado.

It was retro. It was timeless. It was cool.

She took the stairs two at a time, and dashed across the pantry to the kitchen door. There she stopped, and paused for a moment to catch her breath and get herself back under control. She smiled at her own enthusiasm, and suddenly felt a little embarrassed. She could feel herself blushing.

She pulled open the kitchen door, and trying not to sound too excited, she called out to Dean on the other side of the room:

"Hey, Dean, I found someth..."

She stopped in the middle of the word.

The music had abruptly changed, and the person standing on the other side of the room wasn't Dean. It wasn't even a person.

Dean was lying on the floor in a pool of blood, face-down, with his neck bent at an impossible angle. He was quite obviously dead. Crouched above him was a dark and fur-covered animal, almost human in shape, but not human at all... more like a bear, or a great ferocious dog.

Or a wolf... a werewolf.

The monster raised its head and gazed at her from across the length of the kitchen. Shelby stood frozen, her mind struggling to process what she was seeing. She heard the low rumble of a snarl emerge from deep in the creature's throat.

Then suddenly it sprang forward, racing toward her across the kitchen floor. Shelby found her legs, slamming the door behind her as she turned to run. She leapt across the room to the little staircase and scrambled down the dusty wooden steps.

It was not a reasoned choice. She had reacted by instinct, and instead of fleeing along the little corridor into the unknown, she retreated down the staircase to the wine cellar, a place she'd already explored. But that was a dead end, a series of rooms with no other exit, and now she was trapped.

But she knew where she was going: the heavy steel door of the chemistry lab. Her only thought was to get safely behind it. Any plan beyond that would have to wait.

She heard a splintering crash in the room above, and knew that the creature had broken through into the pantry. Shelby dashed under the archway and smacked the glowing button next to the laboratory door. The airtight seals disengaged and the door slid briskly open. She hurried through, and it slid shut again behind her.

She looked down at the door's control panel and her heart sank. It was identical to the panel outside; it had only one button, and nothing else. There was no lock! She had no way to secure the door. She couldn't even pile things against it, as it slid to the side, instead of swinging inward.

Shelby listened intently for any sound beyond the closed metal door. The music was softer now... softer but pulsing with intensity... a desperate rhythm, taut and relentless. Shelby backed slowly away from the door and down the short flight of steps to the main floor of the lab. Her heart was pounding, but she had not given up all hope.

If only the creature didn't understand how to work the door, she still had a chance. She was sure it couldn't break the door open, if only it wouldn't somehow brush against the button by accident she would still be safe. If only her luck would hold.

But even as these thoughts raced through her head, she heard the pressure seals release, and an instant later the door slid to the side.

Her luck had failed her.

The monster took a half-step forward into the open doorway, and from the elevated platform it gazed horribly down at the defenseless young woman standing in the center of the laboratory floor. Staring her own death in the face, Shelby's only thought was that she needed a weapon, any weapon at all. But in the spotlessly antiseptic chemistry lab there was no conventional weaponry anywhere to be found. Acid might harm the creature, or a Bunsen burner might set it on fire, but neither would be quick enough to save her. She would be dead long before the monster was injured badly enough to stop its attack.

With no better options that she could see, Shelby grabbed an amber-colored volumetric flask, and clutching its long neck tightly in her fist she smashed the globular end against the laboratory workbench like an angry drunk smashing a beer bottle on a barstool in a tavern brawl. The chemical solution it had once contained spattered onto her hand, across the workbench, and all along the white-tiled floor.

Never before in her life had Shelby Oswald found herself in a really serious fight. But she'd been on the first team cheer squad since her freshman year of high school, and had seen more than one Quentin Tarantino movie. She was fit and agile, and had a passing familiarity with the concept of brutal, gratuitous violence. She set her feet apart and bent her knees into a ready stance. Drawing her elbow back at shoulder height, she brandished the jagged end of the flask in her right hand, staring down the fanged and drooling monster the same way she might have glared at a blind date gone terribly wrong.

"All right, you furry son of a bitch," she muttered fiercely. "Bring it."

The monster took another slow step forward. Its eyes were smouldering with bloodlust, and the hatred of uncorrupted things. But there was something else there as well, something that looked to Shelby almost like indecision... uncertainty...

Then suddenly, it turned and ran. The steel door slid shut behind it and Shelby heard the pressure seals re-engage.

It hadn't attacked. For some unfathomable reason, the monster had actually run away.

Shelby Oswald had survived Chapter Nineteen after all.

Chapter 20:
Now What?

Shelby was furious.

The werewolf had suddenly run away, just when it had her cornered, and Shelby had no idea why. But now, in the immediate aftermath of that life-or-death moment she wasn't feeling terror, or relief, or joy, or any of the hundred other emotions she might well have been expected to feel.

Instead, she was absolutely incensed with anger.

A werewolf?... *Seriously*?

She and her classmates had endured a brutal semester, studying obscure and arcane mythologies from almost every culture across the globe. They'd examined folk histories and rumors and legends originating everywhere from Namibia to Japan, from Argentina to Alaska, from New Zealand to the Faroe Islands. The class had been assigned over a thousand pages of reading a week, often untranslated, and sometimes in languages Shelby had never even heard of. Just to complete the footnotes on her mid-term research paper, she'd had to learn the formal syntax of Akkadian cuneiform.

And that was just the reading. There were also all the movies they'd studied, covering a century of cinematic horror. They'd run statistical analyses of cross-cultural symbolic constants. They'd researched the psychology of nightmares, including their impact on everything from space exploration to grocery shopping. They'd studied robotics and artificial intelligence, UFOs... the list was endless. The class had covered such a dizzying array of topics that Shelby couldn't even hope to recount them all.

And after all of that, their final exam was a god-damned *werewolf*? **Everyone** knows about werewolves. Shelby had known about werewolves for as long as she could remember. Even her six-year-old cousin Marjorie knew how to kill a werewolf.

Shelby plopped herself down on a stool beside one of the laboratory workbenches, and took a few moments to get her seething indignation back under control. She was no less outraged than before, but she understood full well that – as with fire and robots – anger is an excellent servant but a terrible master. Getting mad about her professor's choice of test materials wasn't going to solve anything: what she had to do now was *think*.

The first question in her mind was *Why did it run away?*... she didn't have an answer for that. Once the werewolf had opened the sliding steel door, Shelby had been sure that her goose was cooked, and there was nothing left for her to do but to go out fighting. The thing hadn't hesitated to charge at her from across the kitchen, so why did it hesitate in the doorway of the lab? Why would it turn and run?

She looked down and saw that she was still clutching the long neck of the volumetric flask in her right hand. In the frenzy of the moment, she'd forgotten all about it. The broken end of the flask was sharp and jagged, and certainly looked very dangerous – maybe even deadly – but would that have been enough to scare off a stalking werewolf? It didn't seem likely.

Then Shelby realized that there were some ugly dark splotches on her hand and arm. When she'd smashed the flask, the liquid inside of it had gone everywhere, and some of that stuff must have spattered onto her hand. At first she was alarmed; there was no telling what sort of acid or toxic solution the flask had once held. She prodded at the dark patches cautiously with the fingers of her other hand, but there was no pain; whatever it was, the stuff didn't seem to have actually burned her skin, or to have hurt her in any way. It was more as if she'd just gotten some ink on her hand, or spilled the toner from a print cartridge.

She carefully set the broken remnant of the flask down onto one of the tables and took a closer look at it. The first thing she noticed was that it was made from dark amber-colored glass. That was odd. The volumetric flasks that Shelby had used in her chemistry classes were all made from *clear* glass, but this was almost the same color as a beer bottle. She wondered why.

Shelby stepped over to the bench where she'd first smashed the flask, and carefully examined the smaller pieces. She could see now that there had been something written on it. She carefully collected all the fragments that she could find, and once she'd reassembled a few of them she could read where someone – presumably Doctor Grimdeath himself – had at some point scribbled a chemical formula on the side of the flask with a wax pencil. It read: $AgNO_3$.

"Silver Nitrate," Shelby said aloud, and suddenly everything made sense.

Almost.

Shelby knew that silver nitrate – or a similar silver compound – had been used to make the original black and white camera film. It was sensitive to light, which explained why it was being kept in a dark glass container, and why her hand had turned dark where it had splashed onto her.

But was that what had scared the creature away... silver nitrate?

The classic way to kill a werewolf, of course, was with a silver bullet. But this wasn't a bullet; it wasn't even pure silver, it was just a bunch of silver ions dissolved in solution. According to some legends, the merest touch of silver would *burn* a werewolf, though other accounts never mentioned silver at all. But even if silver ions in solution would still be dangerous to the monster, how would it have known? Even Shelby hadn't realized what the chemical was at the time, and she was the one holding the flask in the first place.

Could the monster *sense* the silver? That didn't seem likely either. And in any event, by the time it retreated there was hardly any solution left; maybe a few stray drops were clinging to the broken shards of the flask, but otherwise it had already been spilled all over the lab bench and the tile floor.

Shelby found herself wondering if maybe she didn't know as much about werewolves as she'd thought she did. The class had covered them, certainly, at various points over the course of the semester, but now that she thought about it the things they'd learned had left them with more questions than answers. Shelby wasn't even sure about how someone *became* a werewolf. Did you catch it from a bite, like a disease? Or was it more akin to some sort of a curse; or even a deliberate transformation, like an act of witchcraft? The various legends often disagreed on the important details. Sometimes they flat out contradicted each other.

And thinking of those contradictions, Shelby felt a sudden knot twisting in her stomach: her classmates still might not even know what the monster *was*, much less that it was terribly, terribly real, and not merely hypothetical as most of them had believed. Shelby had been so consumed by her own brush with death that she'd forgotten all about her fellow students. It was an understandable lapse, but she couldn't help feeling guilty about it all the same: hers wasn't the only life in danger. Dean was already dead, and for all she knew so might be the whole rest of her class. She shuddered at the thought, and clenched her fists with a fresh sense of resolve.

But above all of her uncertainties, Shelby now felt certain of one thing: silver was important. She could think of no other explanation for why the creature had hesitated... no other reason for why it hadn't simply attacked and killed her outright.

And she also strongly suspected that a few trace drops of silver nitrate on a shard of broken glassware would not be enough to fend the creature off a second time. If she wanted to survive the night, she would need to find a much better weapon – one that was really made out of silver.

Chapter 21:
Search and Research

Meri and Liza immediately set about searching the library for further evidence that might confirm or refute their guess that the monster was indeed a werewolf. It didn't take them long. In the pile of books which Meri had once dismissed as a random assortment of children's stories, a common theme now became obvious. All the books on that table – From *Peter and the Wolf* to *The Three Little Pigs*, and even *Doctor Jekyll and Mr. Hyde* – had been bookmarked or left lying open to stories involving either a wolf or some sort of dire human transformation. The pieces seemed to fit neatly together.

Feeling confident in their conclusions, Liza and Meri agreed that the obvious next step would be to let everyone else know. In fact, they thought it would probably be a good idea for the entire class to regroup, and discuss what they'd each managed to figure out so far. They had little doubt that some of their fellow students would have made significant discoveries of their own.

"So..." said Meri, "the foyer? I'm pretty sure that's where Monroe was headed."

"Hard telling where he went to," Liza said. "Maybe a wrong turn at Albuquerque, but yeah... the foyer's the obvious place to start looking."

Though neither Meri nor Liza had quite realized it, now that they had a working hypothesis for what sort of monster they were up against, their attitudes toward their current situation had dramatically changed. Whereas before they'd been anxious or even fearful that they might be in imminent physical danger, both of them had now begun to treat their final exam as a harmless – if somewhat esoteric – research project. Somehow, having decided what the monster was (or at least what it was supposed to be), had made it seem less *real* to them. That sense of uncertainty which had kept them balanced on the razor's edge between reason and terror was suddenly swept away, and they both – quite unconsciously – had begun to regard their current situation not as a tangible crisis of deadly peril, but rather as just another routine academic assignment.

This, of course, was a mistake.

They left the library by way of the doors that opened into the main hall. From there, they went in opposite directions, to make certain that they wouldn't miss anyone else who might be roaming around on the upper floor. Knowing that the hallway formed a complete loop, they agreed to meet up again along the balcony overlooking the foyer.

Liza briefly checked each door she came to before moving on, but found no sign of the other students. Behind one of the doors she did find a narrow staircase going down, and though she was sorely tempted to find out where it led, she only went as far as the first step before turning back. It was, in fact, the same little staircase that Dean had discovered earlier, leading down to the servants' mess and the mud room. But Liza didn't have time for any detours; she knew Meri would be waiting for her.

"Don't pull a Monroe," she said aloud, shaking her index finger sternly in the air as if she were scolding herself. She smiled inwardly at her own dumb joke, closed the door, and continued on down the hallway.

Meri was even less thorough in her search than Liza was. She tapped on the first couple of doors she came to, to see if anyone was there, but she didn't actually open them to make certain. Now that she was by herself again, she was feeling a little less secure than she had been only a few moments before, and the further she went along the hall the more uncomfortable she became. The shadows at every corner were starting to creep her out again, and without entirely realizing it she'd begun walking a little bit faster and looking over her shoulder a little more often. By the third door, she'd already made the executive decision that if a door was closed, that meant no one would be inside, so she didn't really even need to knock, or investigate it any further.

The only door she found that was standing open was the one leading into the quaint little bedroom she'd explored earlier. She peeked inside, and seeing the colorful pile of pastel tuxedos scattered across the bed brought a smile to her face. However, the sight of the closet where the tuxedos had been hanging still made her feel uneasy somehow, even though that door was standing wide open as well, and she already knew that the closet was harmless and mostly empty.

She scurried the rest of the way down the hall to the foyer, and arrived there well before Liza did. She peeked over the bannister at the entryway, but seeing no one there, she stepped away from the railing and walked as calmly as she could to the other end of the balcony to wait for Liza, who arrived only a few moments later. Meri let out a relieved sigh when she finally saw her, and realized that she'd actually been holding her breath.

"Sorry," she said, looking down at her own feet with embarrassment. "Still a little scared, I guess."

"What happened here?" Liza asked, looking over the rail at the foyer below.

Meri looked down again, and saw the same wet and muddy mess that Monroe had come upon earlier. The front doors were closed, a fire was burning in the fireplace, and there was a sizable puddle of water just inside the entryway. The mud that had been tracked through the room – particularly those patches of it that were near to the fire – had begun to dry up into little dusty clumps.

The two young women were halfway down the curving staircase when the grandfather clock began to strike the hour. It was now ten o'clock. They both stopped where they were, transfixed as if the chimes had magically frozen them in place. But no sooner had the tenth stroke finished than they heard another sound seeping into the room. It was a quiet chorus of strings, playing a haunting melody, somewhere in the distance.

"Gghhrrrr....." snarled Meri.

"Background music," said Liza. "Here we go again."

"It's just to distract us," Meri said. "Every single time we've heard it, it's been a false alarm." Liza nodded in agreement.

It should be mentioned, however, that Liza and Meri's perspective on the music was largely a product of their own agitation (for which the music itself was at least partly responsible). Consequently, theirs was neither an objective, nor an entirely accurate assessment. In point of fact, the music was *quite* important – and had been so every time they'd heard it – though its relevance might not have seemed apparent to them at the time.

But be that as it may, despite the unsettling murmur of a string quartet playing all around them, Liza and Meri continued down the stairs to the foyer. They were both determined to not let the music affect them.

"I guess someone's been outside," said Meri, looking at the puddle of water by the front doors. "And they didn't wipe their feet," she added, looking ruefully at the muddy carpet.

"Well, Monroe's been here, I think..." Liza said. "That's the stick he was carrying, isn't it?" She pointed toward the fireplace, where a very nice pool cue was leaning against the stones.

"Maybe?" said Meri, tentatively. "But why would he leave it here?"

"And hey, look at the candles," Liza said. "Some of them have been lit, but not all of them."

Meri turned to count the candles, but as Lizabel had said, all eight were still there, though only three of them were burning.

"Maybe the other ones blew out when somebody opened the door," Meri suggested.

"I don't think so," Liza said, as she walked across the room to look at one of the unlit candles more closely. "This one's never been lit at all. The wick's still white; it's a brand new candle."

Meri frowned and crossed her arms pensively, but didn't say anything. The two women paced slowly around the perimeter of the room, looking for any clue as to where the others might be, and trying to decide where they should try to look next.

As she passed an open arch leading to one of the mansion's interior hallways, Meri noticed something else.

"Liza?..." she said, hesitantly. "There's a door standing open over here."

Chapter 22:
Light and Shadow

Carson and Rodney were halfway back up the hill to the mansion, when Rodney suddenly stopped.

"What's up with these lights?" he asked, looking over at one of the antique lamp posts that stood beside the path.

"Hmm?..." said Carson, puzzled. "Looks all right to me."

"It's not," said Rodney. "It's different. Look how bright it is. Remember when we first got here? The whole group; we talked about it. The lights closest to us got dim, while the next one up the path ahead of us was brightest. But now, it's the one *next to us* that's brightest, and all the rest of them are lower... like at half-level on a dimmer switch. It's the opposite of what it was before."

Carson looked up and down the path, and saw that Rodney was right. It *had* been the other way before. But he couldn't think of any reason why that would be important.

"Maybe it fixed itself...?" he suggested, "...the storm tripped a breaker or something and the system just did a reset; like rebooting a laptop."

Rodney frowned, and squinted at the lights further up the hill toward the house. He didn't like it... as Rodney saw things, any change at all was a cause for concern. He couldn't think of any good reason why the lights changing would matter, but they *had* changed, and that bothered him.

"OK," he said eventually. "At least I'm not crazy. So they *are* different."

"Yeah," said Carson. "I think so, but I don't think it's a big deal. Stuff gets broken all the time."

They continued up the hill, but as they were approaching the mansion they stopped again. This time, it was Carson who'd spotted something of interest.

"What's that light over there?" he asked, pointing toward the side yard. "That wasn't there before, was it?"

"It's a gazebo or something," Rodney replied. "I saw it earlier, but it was raining too hard."

"Let's go take a look."

"I'd rather get back inside where it's warm."

"Don't be a wimp," Carson said, jokingly. "The rain's stopped, and we're already soaked. This will only take a second."

Shelby took a long while, carefully searching the chemistry lab, but she did not find anything that seemed immediately useful. She'd been more than half-hoping that there might be another bottle of silver nitrate in the room, or even some actual silver, waiting to be dissolved, but she found nothing along those lines. There were some acids and bases, and other common chemical components, but nothing that seemed obviously useful in terms of her current circumstances.

But Shelby had another reason to take her time searching the lab: she was afraid to leave. She certainly hoped that the monster had really fled, that it had run off into the woods or gone elsewhere in the house, but that was far from certain. She knew it might well have just retreated to the wine cellar, where it could lie in ambush, waiting for her to emerge from the well-lit and silver-nitrate-stained laboratory.

But by the same token, she couldn't stay in the lab forever. There was nothing else useful that she could accomplish there now, and she had to get out and warn the others if she possibly could. If only she could make it as far as the pantry, she thought, from there she'd at least have more than one choice of escape routes. If only she could make it up those stairs, her odds of survival would drastically improve.

And as Shelby thought through her limited range of options, she realized something else: she didn't really want to escape. Saving her own life wasn't going to be good enough. She didn't just want to get away from the werewolf, she wanted to *kill* it, like it had killed Dean. Like it had wanted to kill her, and like it was going to kill *everyone*, if she or the rest of her classmates were not somehow able to stop it.

This had nothing to do with her final exam, or earning a high grade in a class. This was something much more than that. It was personal now.

She took the neck of the broken flask in hand again – it was still the best weapon she had – and climbed the little flight of steps to the landing by the door. She took a deep breath, and pressed the little glowing button on the control panel. The door slid open.

Silence.

She stood there for a few moments listening, her muscles taut with anticipation and fear, but there was nothing there. The space beyond seemed even darker than before, and the shadows more harsh. Shelby realized that the only light in the wine cellar now was what was spilling in through the open doorway from the lab. The light bulb overhead had either been turned off or broken.

The door slid shut again, with Shelby still inside the lab. It was automatic, and would only stay open long enough for someone to pass through, or if someone was to stand there, as the monster had, blocking the doorway.

Shelby didn't relish the thought of trying to get through the wine cellar in the dark, not even under ordinary circumstances, and certainly not with a werewolf lurking about. She climbed back down the little flight of steps, picked up a stool from beside one of the lab benches and carried it up to the landing. She pressed the button on the control panel again, and set the stool inside the open doorway to keep it from closing.

She peered cautiously into the room and listened intently, but she saw and heard nothing. It dawned on her that there wasn't even any music playing. Shelby took that as an encouraging sign, and now that the door was propped open there was enough light that she could see her way to the open arch that led into the rest of the wine cellar.

As quietly as a field mouse sneaking through an animal shelter, Shelby Oswald crept out of the brightly lit doorway and into the shadowy gloom.

Carson and Rodney covered Shondra's body with their jackets, and stood shivering for a few moments in the gazebo. A light wind was now blowing out of the west, and the chill of it cut through their damp clothes.

Neither of them had much to say. Once they'd found Shondra, or what was left of her lying there in the gazebo, everything became clear. Even Rodney – who'd already wanted off the island that first minute after the exam had officially started – even *he* knew that they couldn't leave now; not until they'd found the others. No one was going anywhere unless they could all get out together. They both knew it; it didn't need to actually be said.

Badly shaken, but now with a clearer sense of purpose, they scrambled across the darkness of the lawn to the front porch. They saw no one else around, and the entry doors were closed. Rodney silently read the sign again, the one warning them not to ring the doorbell. It had puzzled him earlier, but this time its meaning was abundantly clear.

The two young men stood to either side of the double doors, and Carson pushed open the one that was closer to him. He didn't hear a sound, and nothing came charging out at them through the open doorway. Very carefully, Carson leaned over to look inside.

"Ahh!" he suddenly shouted, and jerked back just in time, as the butt-end of a pool cue missed his head by only inches. The cue smashed against the doorframe and splintered into two jagged pieces.

"Easy! Easy!" Rodney shouted, frantically jumping away from the door and moving further out onto the porch where he could be more easily seen. "It's us! It's us!"

Just inside the entryway were Liza and Meri, both of them brandishing pool sticks and poised to attack. Meri's cue had snapped off against the doorframe, but she was still clutching the nasty-looking shard of the tip end. Even in the poor light, Rodney could see that her eyes were bloodshot; it looked as if she'd been crying.

"Sorry..." she said after a moment's pause, "...didn't know."

"The monster's real," Liza said, relaxing her guard only slightly. "It got Monroe. He's dead."

"So's Shondra," said Carson, stepping cautiously forward into the doorway. "We found her body outside."

Liza bit her lip, and nodded with understanding. She let out a long, slow breath, took a short step backward, and lowered her pool cue.

"Come on inside," she said apologetically, after another moment or two had passed. "Are you guys ok? We think it's a werewolf."

Chapter 23:
A Fireside Chat

Several minutes later, very little more had been said. None of the four students had quite recovered from the shock of finding the bodies of their murdered classmates, and now that the rush of those discoveries had lapsed, they all felt strangely subdued, as if they were somehow constrained to silence.

Carson and Rodney had taken off their shoes, and were sitting on the stones in front of the fireplace, wringing the water out of their socks. Meri was fidgeting nearby, trying to keep watch on all the doors, as well as the balcony and the open archways leading out from the foyer, while Liza added more wood to the fire. It was as if it were too difficult for anyone to speak aloud; almost too difficult even for them to think with words. Though they themselves were only partly aware of it, each of them was feeling the same instinctive desire to do nothing more than huddle silently together in front of the fireplace.

There is something comforting in fire, at least in a well-mannered fire – one that is of modest size, and neatly constrained in a secure enclosure of brick or stone. There is a sort of solace there that goes far beyond the bare physical benefits of light and warmth. There is something primal in firelight, something that reaches beyond our modern sensibilities and our capacity for reason, and brushes instead directly against that latent kernel of Homo Erectus that still lingers in the shared depths of our common ancestry.

Fire helped create us as a species. Over the long millenia it has warmed us and fed us and kept us safe from the myriad dangers of the world. It has enabled us to climb from the lower rungs to the very top of the food chain, and made possible all that we have achieved. For over a million years now, our survival has been tied to it, and in the flicker of its orange and yellow glow, we inevitably feel ever so slightly more hopeful and alive.

"I don't think we can kill it," Liza blurted out suddenly.

This might not have been the best way to start a discussion, but a discussion had to be started, and for the life of her, Liza couldn't think of anything else to say. But it was enough to break the spell of silence that had surrounded them; the others all turned to look at her.

"If there *is* a way we could kill it, I can't think of how..." she continued. "I mean, the pool sticks are the best weapon we've found, and that won't cut it. They were Monroe's idea to begin with, but they didn't do him much good. That's where we found him, was in the billiard room."

"We have *these*," Carson said, holding up his dueling pistol. Rodney held up his as well.

"Where did you find those?" Meri asked, skeptically. "Do they even work?"

"Mine did," said Rodney, feeling a little bit proud of himself. "Shot the lock off of the boathouse door with it. It was a hell of a bang, too."

"One and done, though," Carson admitted. "No idea how to reload it, so we've only got the one shot left."

"I might be able to reload it," Meri said, to the surprise of the other three, "at least in theory I could, if I had all the stuff. It's just a cap and ball musket. It's a pretty simple mechanism, but... well, I've never actually done it. I wouldn't know how much powder to put in, or how tight to pack everything, so... yeah maybe not such a great idea. Sorry. I'm just thinking out loud."

"You'd need a silver bullet, too," Liza pointed out.

"Maybe not," said Meri. "The stuff we read about werewolves was only like 50-50 on the whole silver thing. A regular bullet might be just as good, for all we know."

"I'm guessing that's what's in this one, though," Carson said optimistically.

He slowly raised the pistol, taking careful aim at the suit of armor beside the entryway doors.

"A silver bullet, I mean..." he continued, smiling and lowering the pistol once again. "I mean seriously, otherwise what good would it do, right? The guns were pre-set for the test, after all; the display case

they were in was unlocked, and they were already loaded. So I figure...
it's *gotta* be a silver bullet in there... right? They probably both were.
Otherwise why would he bother?"

Liza didn't share Carson's optimism, but she wasn't going to argue
about it, not when she couldn't suggest anything better. The reality of
their situation was that the group would have to take whatever they
could find and make the best of it. And a loaded gun – even an
antiquated and unreliable one – was obviously a far more promising
weapon than any of their current alternatives.

But now that the silence was broken, the four students quickly filled
each other in on what they'd managed to learn so far. They all agreed
that escaping on the little speedboat was the obvious thing to do,
provided they could find their missing classmates first. With Monroe
and Shondra already dead, that left only Dean and Shelby unaccounted
for.

"We can't split up to look for them," Rodney said, pulling his socks
and shoes back on. He'd made this same point once before and been
ignored, but this time he was determined to get out in front of any
potential argument. "Monroe and Shondra were both alone when they
got attacked," he continued. "I think we're way safer if we stay as a
group."

"Absolutely," Liza agreed. "Werewolves are stalkers; if there's one
thing the legends agree about, it's *that*. Werewolves are sneaky; they
don't go after people in groups, not if they can help it. It's not like
Gojira, or one of the other kaiju stomping through downtown Tokyo
and taking on the whole Japanese army. Werewolves don't want to be
seen. They don't like bright lights or fire. They hang out in the
shadows. They attack from behind if they can, or wait until someone's
all alone, or unwary, or defenseless. They're cowards, really."

"That doesn't help us much," Meri pointed out. "If we're all together
you can bet it'll still come after us. It won't have any other targets."

"You mean *victims*..." Rodney corrected.

"Or *prey*," Liza noted darkly. "And it's true, we're the only game in
town."

"So we've got to find Dean and Shelby... but where do we look?" asked Carson. "They could be anywhere."

"I don't think there's anyone left upstairs," Liza said. "Meri and I did a quick check before we came down."

"I wasn't real careful about it though," Meri admitted.

"I haven't seen either of them since we all split up, right here after the PowerPoint," Rodney said. "I think Dean stuck around though, at least for a little while... to make the fire."

Without warning, the foyer's grandfather clock chimed exactly once. Startled, the students all turned to look.

"Ten-thirty... Liza said, reading the clock. "Shelby was still alive an hour and a half ago. She was with us in the library, but I don't know where she went after that."

"If I know Dean," Rodney suggested, "he'll probably be somewhere around the kitchen, wherever that is."

"Maybe the kitchen is under the library?" Meri said, looking to Liza for confirmation. "Remember?... the dumbwaiter?"

"That's right..." Liza replied, nodding in cautious agreement. "There was a dumbwaiter in the back corner upstairs, so the kitchen's got to be around there too. Somewhere in that part of the ground floor."

As it turned out, finding the kitchen wasn't difficult at all. Carson had already been through much of the ground floor, leaving only one of the hallways from the grand foyer unexplored. Creeping along that corridor the four students soon found the dining room, which was still empty and – had they known it – unchanged from when both Dean and Shelby has passed that way before.

As they drew closer to the kitchen, the atmosphere surrounding the group grew noticeably more tense. Darkly ominous music had begun to play almost as soon as they'd left the foyer, and though it was still very quiet, it had become impossible for them to ignore.

Carson walked in front with his dueling pistol in hand, but he had not yet pulled the hammer back. He felt the danger of the gun going off accidentally was too great to risk keeping it at the ready. He only hoped that if they *did* encounter the monster suddenly, he would have sufficient time to not only cock the weapon, but to aim and fire it accurately.

Directly behind Carson was Meri, still carrying the larger piece of her broken pool cue, and at the rear of the line was Liza, with her own cue stick in hand. Between the two women was Rodney. He was still carrying his dueling pistol, though being empty it was effectively useless now as a weapon. But Rodney found that just having it in his hand was reassuring somehow, and he had nothing else with which to bolster his confidence: he had already completely emptied his water bottle.

Chapter 24:
A Class Reunion

The door to the kitchen was standing slightly ajar, and a clear light was shining from inside. The hinges creaked ever so slightly, as Carson gently pushed the door the rest of the way open. The quiet music that had followed the group from the foyer to the dining room now rose, just a tiny bit, in volume.

From their vantage point in the hallway, the four students did not, for the moment, see anything particularly alarming. The kitchen appeared to be clean and elegant and well-ordered, just like almost everything else in the house. Not until they actually stepped into the room was it obvious that they had come upon the aftermath of another violent encounter.

At one end of the kitchen, where once there had been a wooden door leading to the pantry, there was now only an open doorway, with a few broken splinters of wood still clinging awkwardly to the bent and twisted hinges. On the opposite side of the room, lying just inside another open door was a dead body, face-down in a pool of blood. It was Dean.

Having already discovered Monroe and Shondra in similar states of disrepair, the group had been more than half-suspecting that they might find something like this. But even so, the fact of it still came as a shock. The four students stepped cautiously into the room to investigate further.

"No weapon," Liza said, kneeling down to take a closer look at Dean's mangled body. "No knife, nothing. I doubt he even had a chance to run away or fight; it looks like it got him from behind."

"It was probably hiding there in the pantry," Carson suggested. But Meri was already shaking her head.

"No," she said. "Most of the pieces of that door are on the other side. Whatever broke through there, it was *leaving* the kitchen, not coming in."

"But then why would it break the door down?..." Rodney puzzled, still thinking it through... "Not unless... not unless it was running away."

"More likely chasing after somebody," Liza pointed out.

"Shelby..." said Carson, grimly. "We'd better go look."

The four students gathered around the pantry doorway, and cautiously peered inside. It was Rodney who first caught a glimpse of something moving near the top of the little staircase on the other side of the room.

"Shelby!" he shouted with surprise and relief, once he realized who it was.

Seeing the group on the other side of the doorway, Shelby practically bounded up the last few stairs, and hurried across the pantry towards them.

"I heard you talking from the bottom of the stairs," she said, as she stepped out into the brightly-lit kitchen. "I could hear the music playing up here too, so I was almost afraid to come up," she added, "but believe me, I've never been so happy to hear voices." She took a deep breath, and heaved a huge sigh of relief.

"Thank god you're OK," said Carson. "You were right, there really is a monster; we think it's a werewolf."

"That's exactly what it is," said Shelby, firmly. "I've seen it."

Shelby quickly filled everyone in on her narrow escape, and on what she'd learned in the chemistry lab. But although everyone was eager to hear about her discoveries – and she was just as eager to hear about theirs – the five students took very little time for a thorough discussion. It had already been decided that they should try to escape the island on the speedboat, and though Shelby felt understandably reluctant to give up on killing the werewolf, she wasn't inclined to argue about it. She knew she'd been more than lucky just to survive her earlier encounter with the monster, and certainly didn't have any better plan of action to propose.

"We might be able to kill it, if we had something silver to kill it with..." Shelby said, ruefully. "But there's nothing... nothing I've been able to find anyway. There's no silver in the dining room, or anywhere else that I've looked. Dean said he hadn't been able to find any silverware in the kitchen either, and he was in here for a long time. I'm sure he checked all the drawers and cabinets, probably more than once."

"The other thing that might kill it is *fire*," Liza speculated. "Werewolves are supposed to hate fire, and in some of the legends they were burned at the stake like witches. But I don't see how we can make good use of that. We can't exactly throw the thing into the fireplace. And I'm just going to go out on a limb, and assume that nobody here has a flamethrower."

"I can't think that I've seen silver *anything* in this house," Meri agreed. "Even the doorknobs and the candlesticks were all brass, I think."

"No silver anywhere that I can think of," Carson said. "No torches, either, or anything like that. Lots of old weapons in the trophy room, but they were all iron, I'm pretty sure... not silver. Most of that stuff had some rust on it, and silver doesn't rust."

"It still might be a silver bullet in the gun," Rodney added, hopefully. "But that's a big gamble."

"There has to be *some* way for us to kill the thing," Carson said, emphatically. "Otherwise it wouldn't be a fair test. But you're right, we can't be one hundred-percent sure about the gun, so yeah... I still think we should all get to the boat... like *right now*."

The group backtracked their way from the kitchen, past the dining room and down the corridor to the grand foyer. The quiet pulse of the music followed them as they went, but they saw no sign of the monster. It did not look as if anything else had passed that way recently, or that anything in those rooms had been disturbed in the past few minutes.

According to the grandfather clock in the foyer, it was now 10:49.

As they crossed the open room, Rodney glanced back nervously over his shoulder, and up toward the balcony. He was relieved to see nothing there. It had not been difficult for him to imagine that the creature might have been waiting there, ready to leap down at the group from above. But no, there was nothing, only the tall sweeping staircase and the long balcony rail.

With Carson walking in front, the group passed through the main entryway doors and out to the front porch. The rain had long since fully stopped, and now in the sky above a few stars could even be seen. Before them the front lawn fell slowly away into darkness, broken only by the isolated pools of lamplight that marked the course of the cobblestone path. That path gently wound its way down the slope of the forested hillside, on toward the docks and the boathouse and – hopefully – to their escape.

Chapter 25:
It's All Downhill From Here

"It's watching us," Meri said, glancing up and down the front porch of the mansion nervously. "I can feel it."

"Watching us... *following* us," said Liza, with a hint of resignation in her voice. "But seriously, what else would it be doing?"

"Stay close," said Carson, who was doing his best to project an air of assurance. "We'll all be safer as a group."

"Here's hoping..." added Rodney, who didn't feel nearly so confident as Carson was trying to sound.

The five students left the porch, and cautiously started down the little cobblestone path. Carson, with the loaded dueling pistol in hand, walked in front, while Liza and Shelby brought up the rear, with Liza clutching her pool stick in both hands and Shelby still carrying her broken flask. Rodney, with his own pistol empty, and Meri with the shard of her broken cue, were sticking close behind Carson.

As they worked their way down the gentle slope of the front lawn, the trees ahead of them seemed to close in from either side. The path had not felt nearly so narrow before; not in the evening twilight when they'd first arrived, nor even when Rodney and Carson had gone to investigate the boathouse. The trees were, it should be said, still a good six to eight yards distant from the path, both to their left and their right, and not a single inch closer than they had been before. But perception is everything, and for the moment at least, the trees seemed almost as if they were conspiring to hem them in.

The music followed them as well, across the lawn and down the hill. They had almost grown accustomed to it inside the mansion, but to have it persist into the outdoors, where there was no logical place for a speaker system to be hidden, was decidedly unnerving. Meri wondered if tiny loudspeakers might be in among the trees, or even buried beneath the paving stones of the winding path. She couldn't think of any better explanation.

As they continued down the hill, they saw no sign of the monster. Everyone, however, shared the same certainty that it was stalking them, somewhere nearby. They tried to keep watch in all directions as they walked, their eyes darting ahead, behind, and to either side. More than once, one or another of them stumbled on the uneven surface of the path, as they scanned the island around them, neglecting to keep one eye to the cobblestones below their feet.

They were just passing the lamp post that marked the halfway point between the mansion and the boathouse – and were beginning to hope that they might escape after all – when Shelby, still walking at the end of the line, pulled up short.

"*Wait!...*" she whispered sharply. "*It's in the woods...*"

"*We know...*" Liza whispered in reply, turning back with impatience, and waving her hand to urge Shelby forward. "*Come on, we've got to keep...*"

"*No, **wait!**...*" Shelby said again, even more insistently, and in a slightly louder voice this time. "*It's... right... there.*"

Everyone stopped and turned to look where Shelby was pointing. Directly to one side, in the shadows of the forest no more than a dozen yards away, they could see a dark shape looming. Now that it had been spotted, it slowly slipped forward through the undergrowth, and drew to a halt at the outermost limits of the lamplight.

They could all see it clearly now, and there could be no mistaking what it was. Half man, half beast; a bent and twisted form, with thick dark fur that was black and grey; its lips pulled taut in an angry snarl, its long fangs gleaming wetly with their slightly yellowed hint of ivory-white. The dark heart of the monster's eyes seemed to flicker in the glow of the lamplight with an unearthly scarlet and amber sheen.

"Get behind me!" Carson shouted.

He raised the dueling pistol, and with a sure and deliberate motion, drew the hammer back with his left hand, cocking it. The creature waited, hunched at the very edge of the trees, its eyes fixed coldly on the stout-hearted young man with the gun.

Everything was playing out exactly as Carson had long imagined it. This was the climactic encounter: that one stark moment where the hero stares death in the face, unflinching and unafraid. Carson set his feet apart in his best dueling stance, leveled the pistol at the monster, and waited.

The werewolf's feet did not move, but its head drew ever so slightly backward, and its body seemed to curl itself into a deeper crouch as it prepared to strike.

Carson could feel the universe collapsing around him, disappearing from his mind as his focus, complete and undiluted, fell entirely onto the monster before him. He was aware of nothing else. The forest, the pathway beneath his feet, even the lamplight shining behind him from just above his head, all of these things were winnowed away until nothing remained but himself and the werewolf and the gun.

In that perfect moment, Carson McBride felt himself transformed. He had manifested into the pure and unsullied distillation of every heroic icon he had ever dreamed of becoming. He was John Wayne at the Alamo; he was Custer at the Little Bighorn; he was Alexander Hamilton, staring into the unblinking eyes of Aaron Burr.

He was in the zone.

The creature sprung forward at him, and Carson pulled the trigger. He did not miss. The dueling pistol went off with a deafening roar of smoke and fire, and the bullet flew straight and true, striking the beast full in the center of its chest. The monster lurched in mid-air... in mid-leap. It slumped awkwardly forward, and came crashing down into the muddy dirt, just to the side of the stone pathway.

There was a long hush of stunned silence. The smell of sulphur and saltpeter filled the air, and in the pale glow of the lamplight, wisps of thick white smoke could be seen, curling all around and away from the barrel of the gun.

It had worked. Impossibly enough, real life had followed the screenplay.

Carson McBride had killed the werewolf.

Chapter 26:
Gone with the Win

No one celebrated.

The monster lay motionless at the side of the path. Carson slowly lowered the gun, but otherwise he did not move. No one moved. The werewolf was dead and the eerie music had gone completely silent, and yet none of the five students felt relieved. It had all happened so quickly, so directly; it had been so clean and definitive. They were stunned if anything, still holding their collective breaths. They did not feel triumphant, nor able even to process what had just transpired.

But more than that, each of the five students was now wrestling with some version of the same uncomfortable thought: *it can't have been that easy.*

And of course, they were right.

Carson glanced momentarily over at Liza, who was standing only a few feet up the hill from him. Grasping the barrel of the fired pistol in his left hand, he held the grip out toward her, while also extending his open right hand in her direction as if to say *take the gun, and give me the pool cue.* Liza did exactly that.

With the cue in hand, Carson took a cautious step toward the fallen monster. He could see now that the bullet had gone all the way through the beast; there was a small patch of bloody fur on its back, all around the exit wound. There was no sign that the creature was breathing.

Carson prodded at the body several times with the tip of the pool cue, but nothing happened. He stepped around to the side of the monster, and nudged it again with the toe of his shoe, intending to roll the thing over onto its back.

The body twitched.

Carson stepped quickly backward, raising the pool cue like a club, but the creature did not move again.

"Let's get the hell out of here," said Rodney, who was backing slowly down the path toward the boat dock. Meri, at least, seemed to agree with him, as she had taken a few more steps in that direction as well.

But Carson was determined. He took another cautious step forward, and again jabbed at the body with the pool cue, a little more forcefully this time. When it didn't move, he awkwardly tried once again to roll the thing over with his foot.

That was a mistake.

The body suddenly flailed, and Carson's foot was wrenched violently to the side, throwing him off balance. He fell hard, and tumbled shoulder-first onto the path.

"Run!" he shouted to the others. It was the best idea he'd had in a long time, but he was in no position to take his own advice. He was badly shaken, and could not immediately get his bearings to pull himself back up to his feet. Instead, he scrambled along the muddy stones on all fours, trying to get some distance from the monster, and to give himself a moment to regain his footing.

The creature did not give him that chance. It reached out blindly, and its clutching fingers caught hold of Carson's ankle. The monster was still badly injured, but it was recovering impossibly fast, and rapidly regaining its strength. Already the bleeding had stopped, and the bullet wound had healed itself over completely.

Werewolves, once slain, have an uncanny habit of not staying that way for long. New life was surging within the heart of the beast once more, and with that life came an unquenchable desire to kill. Carson tried desperately to wrench his leg free from the monster's grip, but he could not, and soon the creature was dragging him slowly backwards.

Still hoping he might somehow save the others, Carson fought and kicked with all his strength for as long as he was able. But as for himself, he knew there was no longer any hope at all, and only moments later Carson McBride was dead.

Rodney sprinted down the cobblestone path to the boathouse, with Meri trailing only a few yards behind. By the time Carson had shouted for everyone to run, they both were already running, and neither of them had stopped to look back.

Only when she reached the lamp post beside the boathouse, did Meri turn back briefly to see where the others were. But there was no one there. She blinked her eyes in astonishment, looking back up the hill as far as she could see, but nowhere along that path – not from the spot where she stood to the point where the sparsely-lit trail vanished into the trees – was there anyone else to be seen.

She couldn't believe it. Where was Liza? Where were Shelby and Carson? She had expected everyone to run for the boat just as they'd planned. Even Carson, she'd thought, would have been hot on her heels, once he'd scrambled to his feet again. But in her own panic to get away, she hadn't actually seen which direction the others had gone, aside from Rodney, who was already out ahead of her and leading the way.

Her heart caught in her throat, wondering if the werewolf had gotten them all. Or perhaps the others had scattered into the woods, or back up the hill...? She wiped her eyes with the sleeve of her jacket, turned her back to the hill, and hurried the rest of the way down to the water's edge.

Rodney was already frantically scrambling to remove the tarpaulin from the boat. It was a clumsy effort, as his fingers were ice cold and he was trying not to fall off of the wooden pier and into the lake. Meri had no such reservations. She waded out near the stern of the boat, and standing in the cold, waist-deep water, she quickly freed the tarp from where it had snagged on one of the metal cleats along the starboard side.

Dripping wet, and already chilled to the bone, she clambered over the side of the boat and into the open space behind the seats, just as Rodney was gingerly stepping aboard from the pier.

"Where's everyone else?" he asked, looking back along the path toward the trees.

"I have no idea," said Meri, who did not want to think any more about what might have happened to the rest of their group. "They didn't follow us; let's get out of here."

"Ok... ok..." Rodney said, looking down at the boat's control panel and trying to keep a level head. "How the hell does this thing work?"

"Put on a life jacket," Meri replied, pushing past him to get at the controls. Her chief concern for the moment was *not* to ensure that Rodney was following safe boating procedures, but rather to just get him the hell out of her way.

Because unlike her current companion, Meri knew what she was doing. Her grandparents owned a speedboat very similar to this one – though theirs was quite a bit larger – and as a teenager they'd occasionally taken her out waterskiing with it. She'd rarely been allowed to drive that boat, but she understood the basic controls well enough. She got behind the wheel, pulled the choke, turned the key, and pressed the starter button to fire up the motor.

She heard a click, and a brief *whirrrr....* but otherwise, nothing happened. The engine did not fire.

Fearing the battery might be dead, Meri switched on the boat's headlights as a test. But the battery was good, and the lights came on immediately, flooding the wooden dock with an almost blinding glare. She tried again to start the engine, but the results were exactly the same as before. Desperately, she scanned the gauges on the control panel, trying to figure out what on earth she was doing wrong.

"It's out of gas!" she blurted out in astonishment. "Son of a bitch, it's out of gas!" She pounded on the control panel in frustration.

Meri turned around and looked at Rodney helplessly. They were trapped. The werewolf would follow them down the trail and murder them both. Even if they ran off along the shore or into the woods it would find them, tracking them by their scent. And in any case, it simply wasn't that big of an island. From where they were now they could never make it back to the house, not with the monster lurking somewhere in between; and there was nowhere else that they could hide.

Rodney turned to look back along the cobblestone path, but still he saw no one there. The werewolf had not come after them, at least not yet, and if the others were still alive they had not followed them either, and must have run off to somewhere else.

Still breathing hard from their long run down the hill – and from the chill of the night air, and from fear – he looked back at Meri and then down at the floor of the boat. An idea had come to him.

"Ok...?" Rodney asked uncertainly... "Ok... can you swim?"

Chapter 27:
A Private Chat

Sprinting up the hill toward the mansion, Liza wondered why the hell she was sprinting *up* the hill, and not down the hill as they had all planned. Perhaps it was because at the moment when Carson shouted for everyone to run, the monster had been directly between her and the docks. Or perhaps it was because Shelby – who had been standing right beside her – had started running in that direction first; and in the terror of the moment, with no time to think, Liza had simply followed her out of sheer instinct.

Or perhaps it was for some other reason altogether. Perhaps something inside of Liza already suspected that the prospect of escaping on the boat was just a trap... a lure or a trick or an illusion... a false hope not to be trusted. Perhaps some part of her had already realized, just as she'd thought when Carson first shot the werewolf: *it can't be that easy.*

But whatever unconscious motives had driven her to run back toward the house, by the time she'd reached the mansion's front lawn she had finally put the pieces together. She'd had her epiphany. She had figured it out.

Shelby stopped running, halfway up the yard in front of the mansion, and dropped to one knee. A moment before she'd been in a state of near-panic. In her haste to get away from the monster, she'd even flung aside her only weapon – the shard of the broken laboratory flask – just so she could run that tiny bit faster without the added risk of slicing herself to ribbons.

But halfway across the yard, at the very summit of her fear, she had come quite abruptly to a startling realization, and it stopped her dead in her tracks. It was something so simple and so obvious that she could hardly believe she'd not thought of it before. Everything became suddenly clear to her, the bigger picture burst sharply into focus, and with that flash of clarity, the terror which had almost overwhelmed her dissolved again.

Now she was out of breath and nearly exhausted, but her fear had almost completely faded. All at once, she found herself becoming more rational, and far more keenly focused than she had been only a moment before.

Liza soon caught up to her and promptly doubled over with her hands on her hips, trying to catch her breath as well. Both women turned to look back down the trail behind them, but it did not seem – for the moment at least – that they were being pursued.

"It's not been a fair test..." Liza blurted out, between gasps.

It was the sort of observation that might easily have been the winning entry in an *Understatement of the Year* contest.

"Back when we first got here..." she continued "...when that PowerPoint came up... I realized it then, but I didn't think it all the way through... *we're not his students...*"

Shelby raised her head, and the two women looked at each other for a long moment, both of them still panting for air. Liza continued:

"...We're not the ones being tested. We *are* the test... we're the victims... just so he could test his werewolf..."

"No..." said Shelby firmly, looking down at the ground again and shaking her head. "That's not right... It's not Doctor G's werewolf."

Liza gave Shelby a long, puzzled look. She didn't understand what she was getting at. Shelby straightened up, and clasped the fingers of both hands together behind her neck. She was still trying to get her wind back, trying to get her breathing under control so she could talk, and all the while slowly shaking her head from side to side.

"It's not his werewolf," Shelby continued. "He *is* the werewolf. We were never supposed to kill it. He did everything he could to make sure we couldn't... that we wouldn't be able to. Because it's him... This was all a setup. We were never supposed to figure out how to win, or even how to get away. That's why the boat isn't going to work either. He's probably down there killing Rodney and Meri and Carson right now. That's how he planned it from the very start. We were always supposed to lose. It's been a stacked deck, every step of the way."

Still breathing heavily, Liza shut her eyes, and tried to wrap her head around what Shelby was telling her. It almost seemed impossible, and yet it made perfect sense.

"And that's why there wasn't any silverware..." Liza added, astonished at her own realization. It all seemed so obvious to her now. The myriad bits and pieces of the larger puzzle all seemed to magically snap into place.

"And that's why the guns were already loaded with ordinary bullets..." Shelby continued, pointing to the empty pistol that Liza was still carrying in her right hand. "So if we tried to use them, they wouldn't work. Or rather, they *would* work, or at least they'd seem to, but when it really mattered they wouldn't do us any good."

"Of course..." Liza agreed. "You're right. Of course, you're right. Werewolves heal like a sonofabitch. That's why in so many legends they kept coming back after they'd already been killed. Not until somebody cut the thing's head off, or set it on fire or something."

"Or shot it with a silver bullet," Shelby said. "When it's wounded with silver, it doesn't heal. That's why silver is so important, and that's why the legends don't all agree. Not everybody figured the silver thing out, so they had to make do with whatever else they could. They had to burn the werewolf up, or chop it into pieces so that it couldn't heal."

"So that means Grimdeath knew all along that we couldn't really kill him," said Liza, still thinking it through. "He went out of his way to make absolutely *sure* we wouldn't be able to kill him. We were set up all along to fail. *He planned to kill us...* That rotten bastard, he planned to kill all of us, right from the very start."

"Probably from the start of the semester," Shelby added. "Maybe before that, even. It might be the only reason he wanted to teach the class at all."

"We have to kill him," Liza said, straightening up, and staring Shelby directly in the eye.

"I think it's the only way," Shelby agreed, "and by the same token, I think *he* has to kill *us*. I mean he absolutely **has** to. Now that he's come this far, he can't let us survive the night. He can't leave any witnesses."

"So that means we can't just wait him out, and hang on for the sunrise; he'll have planned for that..." Liza said, doing her best to puzzle everything through from her murderous professor's perspective. "Of course he'd have planned for it... he'd have something else to fall back on. I mean, if he's really testing himself as a werewolf, he'd have to have some other way to kill us, just in case the werewolf thing didn't work out."

"Exactly," said Shelby, bitterly. "If we're still alive in the morning, he might just take out a gun and shoot us."

"I don't see how he'd need a more complicated back-up plan than that." Liza agreed. She turned to take a quick glance back down the path behind them, but still there was no sign that they'd been followed.

"So the only way we can beat him, is if he thinks he can still kill us as a werewolf..." Shelby said. "The only way we can actually kill him... the only way we'll even get a chance to kill him... is to make absolutely certain that he believes we *can't*."

"That shouldn't be too hard," Liza said. "Because right now, I'm not aware of any way that we *can*."

Chapter 28:
In the Absence of a Plan

With no workable plan for how to kill the werewolf – or even a plausible way to escape from the island – Shelby and Liza soon agreed that there was nothing for it but to continue searching the interior of the mansion, in the unlikely hope that a solution would present itself. Once that decision had been made, the two young women turned their backs to the forest once more, and hurried the rest of the way up across the soggy lawn to the mansion's front porch.

Liza cautiously pushed open one of the front entryway doors, and slipped as silently as she could back into the grand foyer. Shelby followed her, and after a quick glance back down toward the forest to make doubly sure that they were not yet being pursued, she very carefully closed the door again behind them.

There was no one else in the room, and no sign that anyone else had been there, not since they'd passed through with the other students only a few minutes before. The fire was still burning brightly in the fireplace, and casting a welcoming glow over much of the surrounding area. But aside from their own breathing and the occasional crackle of burning wood, there was not a sound to be heard. No sound, that is, except for the stopwork mechanism of the grandfather clock, slowly advancing:

chik... chok... chik... chok...

In the great hollow chamber of the grand foyer, that relentless thrumming of the antiquated timepiece seemed almost to echo around them.

"11:06," Shelby said, reading the time. Her voice was not much louder than a whisper. "Whatever we're gonna do, I'd take a bet that we've got less than an hour left to do it."

Liza frowned, and nodded her head in agreement. Given their professor's well-known penchant for high drama, it seemed almost certain that he would aim for a midnight finish, in classic horror style.

For Doctor Grimdeath – meticulous evil genius that he was – his students fully understood that nothing less would do. This meant that if Shelby and Liza were to have any chance at survival, any chance at all, they would have to find a workable solution to their deadly peril sometime before the clock struck twelve.

Midnight was to be their witching hour; the dark side of high noon; the long-appointed end of their magic pumpkin. At midnight, the metaphorical ball would drop from the heavens, right on top of them. Their race against time would be over. The headless horseman would bar their way across the covered bridge, and Cinderella would get eaten.

This was an unpleasant fact, and something which neither of them felt any great desire to dwell upon at the present moment.

"Look at the candles," Liza muttered. She reached out her arm, gesturing toward the metal sconces that were mounted along the room's interior wall. "When we left, only three of the eight were burning; but now there's *four*."

Shelby looked around the room, and tried to think back to the other times she'd passed through the foyer. Had any of the candles been burning then? She didn't think so, but at the time she hadn't really paid much attention, and now she couldn't remember for certain one way or the other. But in either case, there was no disputing Liza's arithmetic, though Shelby wasn't at all sure what she was getting at.

"He's counting us down," Liza explained, in answer to Shelby's unspoken question. "I'd noticed before that only some of them were lit, but I just now figured out why. The candles are there for him to keep score. He lights another one every time he kills one of us."

"But how would that work?" Shelby asked.

"What do you mean?"

"I mean, how could he light them?" Shelby asked again. "I'm not saying you're wrong, but he couldn't have come past us, could he?... not without us seeing him. So how did the fourth candle get lit?"

"That's a good question," Liza replied, as she carefully set aside the empty dueling pistol, leaving it on top of the fireplace mantle. "Let's take a look and find out."

She tried to take one of the candles down from the wall, but found that this was surprisingly difficult to do. The candle clung firmly to its mounting, almost as if it had been bolted in place. Liza couldn't simply lift it out of its holder; she had to twist the whole candle sideways from the top, just to create enough leverage to pry it free.

Once she'd finally separated the candle from its metal base, she could see what the trouble had been.

"Look at this," she said, holding the hefty candle up so that Shelby could see the bottom end. "Electrical wire. He's run these little wires from the wall mounts, up through the middle of the candle, and all the way to the wick. It's an igniter, just like on a gas stove."

"So he wouldn't need to be here," Shelby said. "He could do it all by remote control... I wonder how much of the house is like that? If everything's automated, he can probably run this whole place right from a smartphone. The candles, the lights, the *music*... who knows what else?"

"And if I'm right about the candles," Liza pointed out, "that means he's already killed somebody else."

"But it also means he didn't get everyone," Shelby added. "At least not yet."

The two women looked at each other for a long moment. They were both thinking the same question, but neither of them wanted to be the one to ask it: *What do we do now?*

"We're wasting time," Liza said. "I don't know what else to do but keep looking. Where should we start?"

"Well, I've already done the basement, and you've already done most of the upstairs," Shelby said. "We don't have time for everything, so let's try to hit as much of the ground floor as we can."

"And maybe we should try to stay close to the foyer?" Liza suggested. "If anybody else does manage to get away, they might try to come back here."

"How about that door there?" Shelby asked, pointing toward the front righthand corner of the room. "I haven't been that way."

"It's as good a place to start as any, I guess" Liza replied with a nod.

As luck would have it, trying that particular door would prove to be a very good decision indeed. For the door Liza and Shelby had chosen was none other than the one that opened into the little parlor, which Shondra had investigated earlier in the evening. And though Shondra had not thought much of that room at the time, as it turns out the parlor was in point of fact a room that was very much worth exploring.

Chapter 29:
Departures and Discoveries

At the ragged margins of the forest, only a short distance up the hill from the water's edge, the monster was gazing down toward the boathouse. From its hiding place amid the brush, the werewolf could see the speedboat bobbing gently in the shallows, with the bright forward lights of its prow still washing drunkenly across the foot of the long wooden pier. There were, however, no students anywhere to be seen; not in the blinding glare of the boat's headlights, nor in the pale glow of the last lamp post at the foot of the path, nor even in the darkness further along the shoreline in either direction.

But the creature knew that two of its students had been there only a few moments before, and could not have gone far. The monster had been delayed in its pursuit, partly by the pain of its injuries, and partly by the struggle on the footpath with the heroic young actor. But those obstacles were well behind it now: the boy was dead, and the gunshot wound had fully healed just as the creature had known it would; just as it had planned.

Now, the beast was hot on the heels of its next two victims. It could smell them both, their faint aromas still fresh in the cool of the damp night air. In its mind, already the monster could almost taste the savory warmth of their unsullied blood.

In a low crouch, the creature swiftly skulked across the open space between the forest and the boathouse, where it pressed itself tight against the outer wall, just to one side of the shed's little window. Craning its neck ever so slightly, the monster peered inside. But it saw no one there either, only the random clutter of tools and oddments that had been stored along with the boat.

The creature was cautious by preference, not necessity. The students had already seen it, and by now they most certainly understood precisely what they were up against. And having endured the bullet wound and revived, the monster felt well assured of its own invulnerability. It knew that the students had no other weapons available to them which might do it any serious harm. Under the current circumstances, it was an incontestable fact that the creature posed a most grave and imminent danger to the students, but not so the reverse. The unfolding drama had advanced into a new phase, one in which the beast no longer had any real need for secrecy.

And yet, for the prowling werewolf, stealth was its own reward. It lent a sense of challenge, a note of mystery to the night's proceedings, which might otherwise have felt too pat, too predetermined; less like an adventure and more like a foregone conclusion: a weakly anticlimactic climax. And honestly, what fun would there be in that? For the transmogrified evil genius, anything that might add to the evening's atmosphere of suspense and terror only enlivened the game.

The monster crept around the corner of the little shed, and down to the shoreline. Standing now at the water's edge, it could see that the little speedboat was empty. A pair of life jackets lay in the hollow at the rear of the craft, but no other sign of the students remained. The creature slashed at the empty air with a long-fingered hand and snarled quietly with annoyance. Where could they have gone?

The beast raised its head and once again sniffed the night air. The scent was strong; the monster felt certain that the students had been in the boat only a few moments before, and that they had not run off along the shoreline. With no other route of escape open to them, the creature guessed (quite correctly) that the students must have fled out along the pier.

A ferocious wave of elation washed over the beast as it leapt onto the dock and raced out along the wooden decking in full pursuit, certain that it now had its quarry fatally cornered at last.

But at the end of the pier, the monster discovered that its prey was no longer there. Clothes and shoes, along with a broken pool cue and an ornate dueling pistol, all were strewn across the wooden planking. The students had fled into the lake, even without use of the boat. They had chosen to swim for the mainland, to perish from cold and exhaustion, to drown in the dark and icy waters, rather than openly face their appointed doom.

This was a turn of events that the professor had not anticipated, and it came as a bitter, bitter disappointment. Denied his prize, and furious at the injustice of it, the creature bellowed out an unspeakable howl of frustration and rage.

Shelby and Liza found the little parlor exactly as Shondra had left it nearly three hours before. It was pristine, and inviting, and almost impossibly cozy.

"OK..." Shelby said, looking around at the perfectly pleasant surroundings, "this is adorable."

"Meh..." said Liza, unenthusiastically. The ambiance of the room was distinctly at odds with her personal sense of aesthetics, not to mention the underlying vibe of their current predicament. "It reminds me of that bedroom upstairs. The one with the secret door in the closet."

The first part of the room to catch Shelby's eye was the two windows overlooking the side yard. She walked to one of them and took a long look at how the curtains were hung, but nothing about the window treatments seemed either immediately useful or even the least bit out of the ordinary. The hardware all appeared to be made of brass, and the curtains were made of sheer cotton fabric with a simple floral print.

Briefly, Shelby peered out through one of the windowpanes toward the gazebo; but then remembering that Shondra's body would be lying out there somewhere, she quickly turned away and pulled the curtains sharply closed.

Liza picked up a white lace doily from one of the upholstered chairs, then put it back in place, smoothing it neatly flat again with the heel of her hand. She tilted the chair onto two legs to look underneath it, but saw nothing unusual there either. The bottom of the seat was supported with spring steel wire and heavy canvas strapping, but Liza couldn't think of any way that such things might be used to kill a werewolf.

She stepped around the chair to the little rolling cart, and looked over the delicate china teacups and saucers with their matching blue and white teapot. Then she noticed the twelve-piece set of gleaming teaspoons, all neatly wrapped in a white linen napkin.

"Shelby!..." she said excitedly, her voice a taut whisper.

Shelby jumped with surprise, and rushed over to the tea cart to see what the sudden fuss was about. Liza had already dropped to her knees, and was lifting the cart's cloth skirt, to have a look at the storage space underneath. But she did not find what she'd been hoping to find. There was nothing stored on the cart's lower shelf except for an empty wooden serving tray, a few folded towels, and a small stack of spare linen napkins.

"Damn it!..." Liza said, in frustration. "Damn it, damn it!... Nothing!"

Shelby grabbed one of the spoons, and held it up to the light. Looking closely at the back side, near the base of the stem she could clearly read the original manufacturer's hallmarks. In a tiny sans serif font, the spoon had been neatly stamped: "Georg Jensen - 925 Sterling - Denmark".

"These are silver!" Shelby exclaimed.

"And a fat lot of good that does us," Liza said, standing up again. "There aren't any *knives*... Nothing! It's not a full set of silverware; there's just tea spoons."

"But they're sterling!" Shelby said. "These are genuine; they're real silver."

"What can we do with a bunch of spoons?" Liza asked. "It's a werewolf, not a killer sorbet. We can't exactly spoon it to death, can we? And it's not like we have time to melt one of them down into a bullet, even if we had the tools to do it with."

Shelby's excitement crashed headlong into a solid brick wall. She dropped her head and frowned miserably, as the rockslide of her enthusiasm crumbled into the loose gravel of disappointment.

"There has to be something we can do with them," she insisted bitterly, though she knew in her heart that Liza was right. What difference did it make if the spoons were real silver? A spoon is not much of a weapon. And even at that, they could never get close enough to the monster to use them, not without being torn to shreds. She clutched the spoon tightly in her fist and stared at the teacart, trying her best to think. But she just couldn't do it. Unable to come up with anything useful, she blurted out the first thing that popped into her head.

"You know who would love this stuff?" Shelby asked, looking at the teapot and the china cups. "My cousin Marjorie. She's an awesome kid; she's only like six years old, but this would totally be her kind of thing. She loves the girlie stuff, like playing dress-up and dolls and everything like that. And I mean, with this setup?... Wow... We could have ourselves a *killer* tea party. She'd be on cloud nine."

Liza scowled for a long moment with annoyance. She was not in an indulgent mood, and under their current circumstances, she had absolutely no interest at all in Shelby's juvenile cousin, or in playing dress-up, or having tea parties with dolls and stuffed animals.

But sometimes, it is those things which – if left entirely to ourselves – we might never even have considered, that can open us up to new possibilities, and opportunities that might otherwise have gone unimagined. And so it was with Liza at that very moment; for to her great surprise, Shelby's random musings had inspired a radical new thought.

"You know what?..." Liza said, nearly smiling in spite of herself. She stared off into space with her eyes wide, and put both hands on her head. She tugged absently at her own hair in astonishment, as the nebulous vapors of a lunatic scheme slowly began to coalesce in the darkest corners of her fertile mind.

She turned and looked Shelby squarely in the eye.

"That..." she said, "is a *fabulously* bad idea."

Chapter 30:
A Tea Party to Die For

Over the next half-hour, Liza and Shelby scoured the ground floor of the mansion, searching for the things they would need. But unlike their previous explorations, this was no longer a random search for clues, or weapons, or even for inspiration. They knew now what sort of things they were looking for, and in many cases they knew exactly where those things could be found.

First, they rolled the tea cart out from the parlor and into the grand foyer. Then they brought in two of the parlor's upholstered easy chairs, and set them up so that they were facing the foyer fireplace. From the billiard room, they retrieved all the remaining cue sticks, took them apart, and placed the separate halves of each stick on one or the other of the two cushioned chairs.

From the kitchen, they took a long-handled soup ladle, and a fairly large stewpot which they filled less than halfway with water. From the center of the elegant hardwood table in the formal dining room they took the gold-rimmed vase full of wolfsbane flowers.

All of these things, they brought back with them to the grand foyer. There, they added more wood to the fire, and made a flat spot amid the coals to one side where they could set the stewpot to boil. Moving to the foyer's interior wall, they pried all eight of the candles free from their sconces, lit them if they were not already burning, and set them on the floor in a broad half-circle surrounding the fireplace, with themselves, the chairs, the teacart and everything else, all on the inside of the ring.

Next they set out eight of the cups and saucers, placing them on the foyer floor, one set directly behind each of the lighted candles. Holding napkins in their hands so that they would not have to handle the wolfsbane directly, they carefully broke eight individual flowers off of the dining room centerpiece, and placed a single bloom in each of the empty teacups. Then they scattered the rest of the flowers all along the semi-circular arc of the candles. And finally, on a folded white linen napkin beside each teacup, they carefully laid one of the sterling silver tea spoons.

By the time they finally had everything in place, the grandfather clock showed the time as 11:49. Liza hurriedly checked to see if the water in the stewpot was boiling, while Shelby busied herself with the disassembled pool cues, prodding at the stones of the fireplace mantle with them in a rhythmic, ritual motion, almost like a tantric dance. In a low, quietly determined voice, she began to sing the Dume University fight song.

Liza ladled the steaming water out from the kettle in the fireplace, and into the blue and white china teapot. With the water and mud from earlier in the evening still spattered here and there around the room, the net result of Liza and Shelby's labors was an arrangement that looked more than anything like a haphazard amalgam of a misbehaving child's imaginary tea party, and a makeshift shamanistic ritual.

Which is precisely what it was intended to be.

With ashes and soot taken from the stones of the fireplace hearth, they symbolically streaked their arms and faces with sacred tribal markings of power, to ward themselves against all encroaching evil. And with that, everything was almost ready. Their time was short, and swiftly growing shorter, but their preparations were nearly complete. All their ducks were now assembled, if not yet aligned in a perfect row.

Shelby and Liza had a plan, but they did not know if it would work. There was no way for them to determine if it would work or not without testing it first, and there was no way for them to test it other than to give it a shot under live conditions, cross their fingers, and hope for the best. They would only get one chance. There was no time for a dress rehearsal, and if it all somehow went to hell on their first attempt, there would be no opportunity for a second take. They were shoving all their chips to the center of the table, not even sure themselves if they were only bluffing or if they really held a solid hand. It didn't matter. Either way, they were going all in.

But amid the danger and the uncertainty, they were comforted by one thought: their adversary had made mistakes.

They knew that Professor Grimdeath had planted red herrings to confuse and distract them. These included the speedboat and the dueling pistols, and almost certainly many other things which they had never found or noticed. But for all of his scheming, his preparations had been neither flawless nor foolproof. He had seemingly overlooked certain small details, details such as the flask of silver nitrate in the chemistry lab, and (they hoped) the Danish silver tea spoons on the little cart in the parlor.

In a traditional Victorian mansion such as this one, silver furnishings would have been commonplace. Candlesticks, picture frames, snuff boxes, letter openers, match cases, and a thousand other decorative and utilitarian silver trinkets would have been prominently displayed in every room. They would have been found resting on end tables and atop mantlepieces, inside glass-fronted cabinets and anywhere else where they might easily be seen. But in this house there had been nothing of the sort. The professor had removed them all, with that one notable exception.

Liza and Shelby clung to the hope that this one exception was not just another red herring; that it really *was* a mistake on their professor's part, and one which would prove to be his Achilles' heel. If their professor-turned-werewolf was truly afraid of silver – as he certainly seemed to be – then inspired by Shelby's mention of tea parties, and Liza's recollection of the warding circle in the octagonal tower room, they were hoping to use that fear against him.

Doctor Grimdeath was intrigued.

By the time he'd returned to the mansion, his two remaining students were already intently at work on their strange ritualistic project in the grand foyer. He watched them for some time through the video surveillance cameras – fed directly to his smartphone – and though he could not determine exactly what the two young women were up to, it seemed apparent to him that neither of them was going anywhere any time soon. It certainly appeared that they were preparing themselves to make a desperate last stand in the grand foyer, right there in front of the fireplace. And if that was indeed the best plan they could come up with, well then, that was an arrangement which suited the mad doctor's designs perfectly.

He chose some suitably ominous background music, set it to begin playing in the grand foyer, and switched his smartphone off again. Then, unexpectedly finding himself with a few spare minutes in which to make some final preparations of his own, Professor Grimdeath took the opportunity to wash himself off in one of the upstairs lavatories, neatly comb his silvery grey hair (what he still had of it), and attire himself suitably for the occasion.

"Perfect..." he said aloud, as he looked himself over in the bathroom mirror. "This... is going to be fun."

When the hushed and sinister music began to play around them, Liza and Shelby knew that their professor must be somewhere nearby, and was probably watching them closely. With only a few minutes remaining until midnight, Liza began to carefully fill each of the eight china cups with the heated water from the teapot, muttering quietly to herself as she did so with soft words of mystical portent in every language she could think of. Soon, she abandoned words entirely, and found herself chanting meaningless, nonsensical sounds in rhythm with the dramatic music. How could it hurt? Liza could think of no better time or place to cut herself loose from the last remaining shackles of logic, sense or reason, and – like a shaman on a spirit quest, or a slam-dancer in the mosh pit – to fully embrace the sacred juju of feral prelingualism. Why the hell not? Why the hell not indeed.

Still intently focused on her own ritual task with the pool sticks, Shelby could not help but overhear Liza's strange incantations, and soon she began to intone along with her in counterpoint, until their two voices were fully entwined. With the music around them steadily growing in volume and intensity, the two young women sang and chanted and beatboxed the stones of the fireplace right along with it, until the grandfather clock suddenly began to chime.

The music abruptly stopped, and the room fell instantly silent. The two students turned to watch the old clock as it slowly, methodically struck the hour:

One...

Two...

Three...

Four...

Five...

Six...

Seven...

Eight...

Nine...

Ten...

Eleven...

Twelve...

Chapter 31:
I'd Like to Meet His Tailor

"Good evening..."

At the sound of the voice, Liza and Shelby looked up toward the balcony above the grand foyer. Standing there beside the railing at the top of the staircase was not the werewolf they had expected, but their professor, Doctor Grimdeath himself, perfectly coiffured and neatly appointed in a garish lavender tuxedo.

"And congratulations," he added, taking a few casual steps down the staircase towards them, "on the completion of your final exam. The others from your class, unfortunately, have not fared so well."

Liza's heart caught in her throat, and Shelby gritted her teeth. They had held out some hope that at least one, or even two of their classmates might have escaped. But it was apparently not so.

"Does this mean we've passed?..." Liza asked, cautiously.

"Ah..." the professor said, taking a few more steps down the stairs. "Yes... well, about that. I can't help but be curious about... um... all of *this*." He gestured vaguely to the state of the grand foyer. "I love what you've done with the place."

"It's a warding circle," Liza replied. "To keep the werewolf out."

"Since we can't kill it," Shelby added, "this seemed like the next best thing."

"Oh, I see..." the professor replied, as he continued to slowly work his way down the curving staircase.

"Silver spoons..." he noted, his voice betraying only the slightest hint of surprise. "A few candles; some faux tribal war paint; a pair of Victorian easy chairs; a little warm water in some teacups...? A wee bit of everything... how very cross-cultural of you."

"We had to make do with whatever was available," Liza said.

"It's not like we had time to go shopping," Shelby added.

138

Doctor Grimdeath gave his two students a doubtful smile, then paused roughly halfway down the stairs, looking about the room with an increasingly critical eye.

"All the same, it's not a very potent warding circle, is it?"

"I modeled it after the one upstairs in the tower," Liza replied, a little defensively.

"Is that what you thought it was?" the professor asked. "How disappointing. And are these flowers supposed to warn the monster off, or frighten it away?... But you see that was never what the wolfsbane was for."

The professor resumed his slow descent, until he paused once again on the last stair.

"A tincture of wolfsbane, you see, was necessary to the transformation, as was that little shrine you visited in the turret. How does one become a werewolf, after all? How is a werewolf made? It's a daunting question, and it took me *years* to work it all out... A little chemistry here, a little alchemy there, a little black magic now and again on the side. All very low-tech, mind you... considerable trial and error was involved. And it's a dreadful shame, really, but I'll probably never get to publish the research. To be perfectly honest, I have always been more focused on the thrill of discovery than on carefully documenting my experimental processes. And even setting aside the ethical questions that might be raised – concerning some of the testing procedures I've adopted, if nothing else – the replicability of my results is... shall we say *somewhat uncertain*? Even were I to take the trouble to write everything out in great detail, I doubt that such a paper would ever survive peer review."

With the faintest trace of a knowing grin creeping across his lips, Doctor Grimdeath took the final step, down from the staircase and onto the foyer floor. Liza shuffled ever so slightly backwards, moving herself further away from the ring of candles, and closer to the stone hearth and the fire. Her professor pretended not to notice.

"But about this warding circle," he continued, skeptically. "It would seem that you've neglected to consider something fundamental about the nature of werewolves."

He took another step forward to the edge of the Persian rug. Liza inched further back, until she was standing beside one of the upholstered chairs. Shelby, with half a pool cue still in her hands, was standing between the other chair and the fireplace, and had not moved.

"What makes a werewolf different from most other types of monsters?" Doctor G asked. He had meant it as a rhetorical question, and he did not wait for an answer. "A vampire, for comparison's sake, is always a vampire. A zombie is *always* a zombie. A gelatinous slime creature might change shape and grow, but nevertheless, it is *always* a gelatinous slime creature."

"But a werewolf," he said, taking another slow step forward, "*isn't* always a werewolf. Ninety-five percent of the time, it's simply a person... otherwise quite ordinary in almost every way. It only becomes a werewolf when it transforms. And how does such a transformation occur?"

Standing now at the very edge of the ring of candles, he shrugged non-committally, with his palms turned upward in an almost apologetic gesture of resignation.

"That, I'm afraid," he added slyly, "would be telling. I *will* let you in on one little secret though: it has very little to do with the full moon."

And with that, Doctor Grimdeath raised his right foot, and with the toe of his neatly polished two-toned shoe he tipped the candle that was nearest to him over onto its side.

"Oh dear..." he said quietly, and with mock concern. "Your warding circle seems to have been broken."

"Get back!" Shelby shouted, though whether she was warning off her professor or urging Liza to retreat was not at all clear. But it did not really matter which, for Professor Grimdeath had already begun to transform.

The change was astonishingly swift, and horrible to behold. Shadowy vapors swirled about the old man, as his hands and face elongated and his body began to contort and swell. The doctor's mouth twisted with a tortured scream of either anguish or rapture, as the teeth inside erupted to become fangs, fangs which gleamed with the pale and ghastly shade of yellowed ivory. Unable to contain the creature's expanding frame, the lavender tuxedo grudgingly burst apart at the seams and tore itself to shreds, falling in tatters from the monster's massively slouching and hirsute body.

Liza and Shelby did not move. They stood behind the two upholstered chairs as if rooted in place, transfixed by the horror of what they were seeing. Its metamorphosis fully complete, the creature writhed where it stood, flexing the muscles that rippled beneath its skin, as if the professor-turned-monster needed a few additional moments to grow reaccustomed to this more savage form.

Still panting with the exertion of the change that had come over it, the creature snarled ominously, as its gaze swung hypnotically back and forth – first to one student and then to the other, as if it were finding it difficult to choose between these two potential victims – until at last its eyes were locked upon Shelby Oswald.

She was the one that had first defied it, and then had escaped from it a second time. It would not allow her to escape again. She was the one that it would kill first.

With impossible strength and speed the monster sprang forward, over the back of the upholstered chair, striking directly at its diminutive prey.

It was a fatal mistake.

As the creature leapt into the air, fully committed to its attack, Shelby raised the pool cue she had been holding in her hand the entire time, the cue that had been largely hidden from her professor's view behind the back of the cushioned chair. Too late, the monster realized that at the business end of that dismantled half-cue, was one of the twelve silver spoons from the tea cart. The handle of that spoon was tightly wedged into the half-cue's empty wooden socket, and by diligently honing the shallowly-cupped bowl of the spoon against the stones of the fireplace, Shelby had hastily ground it down into a serviceable spearpoint.

It was a crude and inelegant weapon, but it didn't need to be pretty. It only needed to be sharp, and made of silver, and it was both.

The creature impaled itself on the makeshift spear, crashing awkwardly over the back of the chair and onto the stones in front of the fire, as Shelby tumbled clear to one side. Wrenched from her hands, her improvised weapon clattered away across the hardwood floor.

Blood streamed from a jagged gash near the monster's shoulder. It was wounded, but it was far from dead. It struggled to its feet, and again turned toward its chosen prey. Its eyes were fully aflame now, no longer with the sport of the hunt, but with pure hatred and venomous, murderous rage. Shelby backed away, but she did not try to run. Caught in the monster's baleful gaze, she knew that she could not hope to escape.

She didn't need to. In his single-minded fury, the professor had forgotten about Liza. Before he could even gather himself for a second leap, she came charging at him from just behind his line of sight with her own teaspoon spear. This was no glancing blow. Liza had time enough to put all of her strength and the whole weight of her body behind it, and she did exactly that. The spear plunged so deep into the monster's ribcage that the silver tip protruded on the other side.

The creature howled with agony, and its whole body spasmed with rage and pain. Dusky smoke rose from where the jagged silver speartip had pierced it. The monster flailed after Liza, but to no avail. She had leapt away again, and even as it lashed out at her, Shelby recovered her own spear. She circled around to the monster's other side, and finished him at last, with a definitive blow.

There on the stones of the hearth, the werewolf collapsed into a pool of its own blood. As the two students watched with horrified fascination, a greyly vaporous cloud enveloped the body of the beast, and the hideous metamorphosis began to reverse itself. Soon the monster was gone, and all that remained was the naked human form of their former professor, shrouded in an eerie violet glow. That strange light seemed almost to struggle against the flickering amber of the fireplace, until the corpse suddenly erupted into a conflagration of blue and purple flames that swiftly consumed it. A moment later, nothing of the body remained, not even the blood that had been spilled. The two spears fell harmlessly onto the hearthstones.

Doctor Alistair Grimdeath, the evil mastermind and self-made werewolf, might have been larger, faster, and much more powerful than either of his intended victims. But in classic villain fashion, he had underestimated them. It is a grave error to ever discount the genius of youth, and regardless of the circumstances, one must never forget that hell hath no fury like a cheerleader with a sharpened spoon.

The professor discovered too late that his students had never intended for their warding ritual to actually work. The tea party had been a ruse. They had meant it only as a distraction, a red herring to pique their adversary's curiosity, one student diverting his attention while the other sharpened the spears. They had lured him in with a false sense of security, just as he himself had lured them and their classmates to the island in the first place. Deceived with the hubris of his own deceptions, he had been duly hoisted on his own petard.

Epilogue:

For the surviving students, the days and weeks and months that followed their somewhat unconventional final examination were filled with a frenzy of inquiries, inquests, investigations, threatened lawsuits and countersuits, and the looming uncertainty of possible criminal charges. Several students were *dead*, after all, and their attending professor – who also happened to be Dume University's most famous and notorious personage – was nowhere to be found. The legal cliché *under suspicious circumstances* did not seem remotely adequate to describe any part of the situation.

The university's legal team was torn between their reflexive impulse to find suitable scapegoats for the incident, balanced against their eagerness to have the whole mess over and done with as quickly as possible. In the end, no charges were filed against any of the parties involved, and all the pending civil suits were hastily settled out of court. There was, after all, the professor's extensive fortune to be considered; and money has an uncanny way of looking out for itself, and for aligning the wheels of justice accordingly.

Under the terms of the final agreements, each of the deceased students was granted a posthumous diploma with honors from Dume University, and generous scholarship funds were established *in memoriam*, and assigned to the university departments for their respective majors. Each of the four surviving students was also provided with an undisclosed sum, either out of sympathy for their unfortunate ordeal, or as hush money, depending upon whose opinion was asked. And, as Doctor Grimdeath had no heirs and no close relations, once the other various settlements were settled, most of his remaining holdings – at least those for which any official records could be obtained – reverted to the University's general fund as a permanent endowment.

Gregor Karmazoff, the missing doctor's ~~chief accomplice~~ trusted graduate assistant, disappeared shortly after the incident, and was never heard from again. Years later, it would be rumored that he was living under an assumed name somewhere in the Balkans, working as a private contractor for the research department of a major international pharmaceuticals conglomerate.

And yes, as mentioned above there were in fact *four* survivors of Doctor Grimdeath's final exam. Rodney Halifax and Meridian Palmer did not drown, as their professor had so hastily assumed, nor did they foolishly attempt to swim all the way to the mainland across the frigid waters of Lake Panasquana in the dead of night. Instead, wearing life jackets taken from the boathouse, they swam only to the furthest end of the island's little cove. There, out of sight from both the docks and the mansion, they used the tarpaulin from the speedboat to fashion a makeshift tent, and spent a very awkward and educational night together, more than half-naked and doing their best to keep warm under very trying circumstances.

As morning approached, they took turns inflating the enormous Loch Ness Monster pool float, and with the first glimmers of pre-dawn light, they set off across the lake on it. Long before they ever reached the mainland, they were spotted and subsequently rescued by a pair of teenagers, who were out for an early morning joyride on their jet-skis.

Later that summer, Meri accepted a scholarship to the PhD program in Robotics at Stanford. Rodney moved to California with her, and took a job as a computer programmer, working on artificial intelligence systems for a major military contractor. Less than a year after their harrowing escape, Rodney and Meri were legally joined together in the bonds of matrimony, in a pagan ceremony held in Yosemite National Park and officiated by none other than Lizabel Paquero. Shelby Oswald was their maid of honor. Carson McBride was chosen to be their best man, in absentia.

As testament to the adage that opposites attract, Liza and Shelby established themselves as a partnership under less formal, but equally dedicated terms. Shortly after graduation, they moved to England, where Shelby had been accepted as an intern at the British Museum, helping to research and curate their extensive collection of untranslated Akkadian cuneiform clay tablets. Liza briefly took a position as an assistant botanist for poisonous plants at England's Alnwick Garden, until she was able to establish herself in a rewarding private practice as an independent consultant in spectral and metaphysical phenomena.

– The End –

Acknowledgements:

I first developed this story idea quite a few years ago as a game design. It was a cooperative boardgame, where a group of students were trapped in their professor's mansion, stalked by a bloodthirsty monster. I never got around to publishing it, but I loved how every session of that game took on its own sort of narrative. It really played out like a classic horror movie, but one that turned out very differently each time.

In translating that idea from a boardgame to a book, some changes were inevitable. But I also wanted to preserve as much as I could of what made the game fun: particularly the sense of discovery, mystery and humor, all balanced against the lurking potential for a sudden and violent death.

So this book has emerged from a long and somewhat circuitous process, and many people have contributed along the way. With the original game, Doree, Morgen, and Maddy Bedwell were all particularly supportive, both through multiple play sessions and simply with their encouragement and enthusiasm. And I should also mention Meric and Kerri England, who at one point endured a particularly long night of ambush playtesting with patience and good humor.

As for the book itself, the corrections, comments and critiques I've received from my preview readers have been indispensable in improving the clarity and quality of the final text. On that front, special thanks must go out to Mark Hansen, Robert Sartain, Thomas Baumbach, Craig Kilgore, Jason Hayes, Cindy Kessler, Renee Retter, and Sharon Hays. I would also like to thank Amy Nagi for all her work in creating the book's cover art, and for an outstanding collaborative process.

And most of all, I would like to thank you, Dear Reader, for taking a chance on this book, and the little-known independent author-guy who wrote it. The support and encouragement I have received over the years from readers like you are what keep me going.

So thank you. Thank you so very much.

– Doug Bedwell

About the Author:

At one time or another, Doug Bedwell has been a playwright, an actor, a college instructor, a computer programmer, a lighting designer, a factory laborer, a carpenter, a department store clerk, a construction worker, a lab assistant, a landscaper, a summer camp counselor, a pizza delivery guy, and many other vocations too numerous or embarrassing to mention.

Elements of this eclectic background frequently find their way into his creative work. For an artist, nothing is wasted. Every experience – good, bad, or otherwise – becomes one more source of insight or perspective.

His plays have been produced in academic, community, and professional theatres from coast to coast. In 2016, he published his first novel, the science fiction comedy *Robot Captain*, followed in 2018 by the fantasy adventure *A Counterfeit Princess*. He has also published a novelette – *The Stone Troll's Diary* – and a small collection of poetry entitled *Wastewood*.

Doug lives in a secluded patch of forest somewhere in rural Indiana. He has never invited students to his home to take their final exams.

A Counterfeit Princess

Doug Bedwell

Also by Doug Bedwell:
The fantasy adventure *A Counterfeit Princess*

Available from most online booksellers in hardcover, paperback, and e-book editions. Copies signed by the author can be ordered directly from Space Bear Press at **spacebearpress.com** or from our web store at **https://space-bear-press.square.site/**

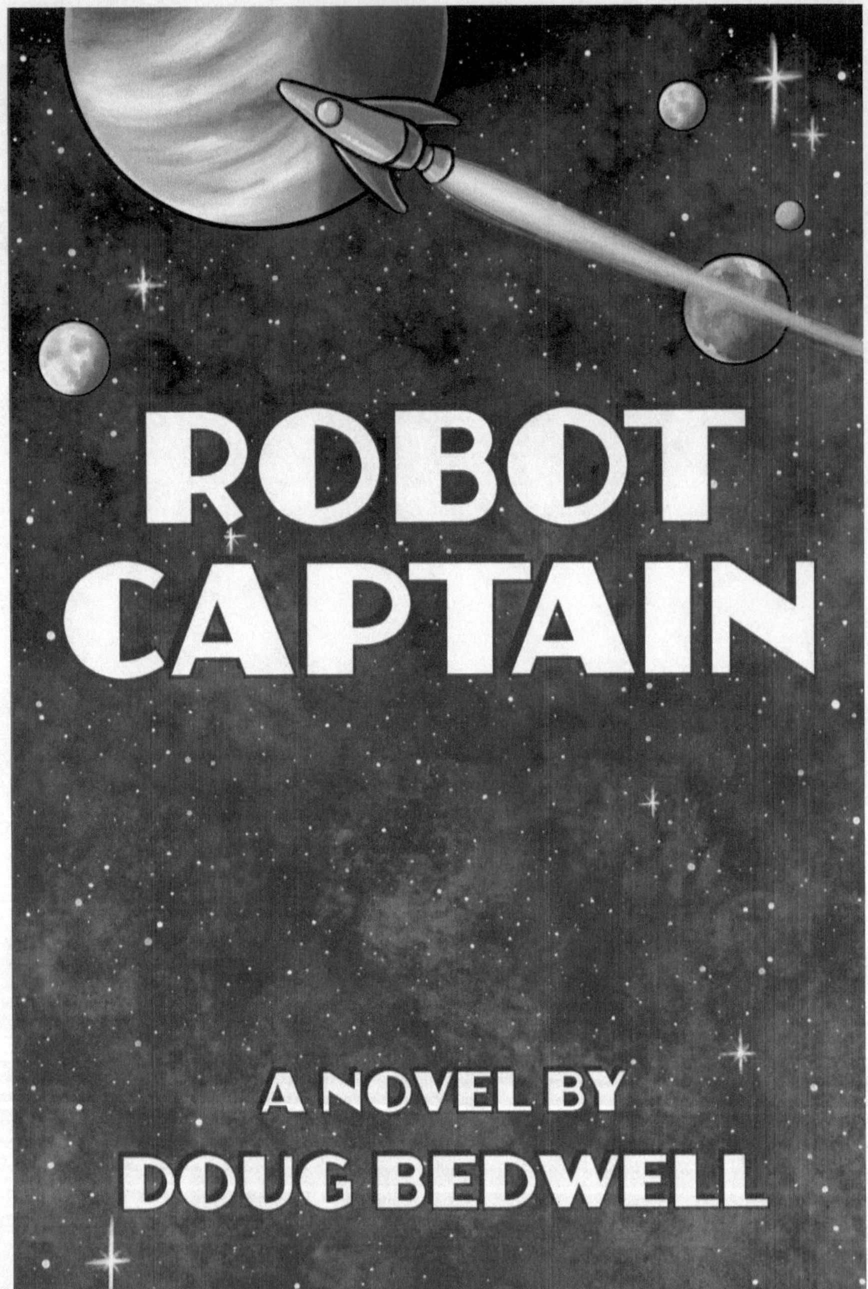

Also by Doug Bedwell:
The comic science fiction adventure *Robot Captain*

Aboard the starship Undertoe, a skeleton crew of misfits takes orders from a smugly bureaucratic computer which couldn't care less if they live or die.

The Undertoe is part of the Galactic Freedom Corporation, a huge interstellar conglomerate whose owner -- the inconceivably wealthy Largo Foote -- has a cunning scheme to seize control of the galactic economy.

Unaware that their ship is a key pawn in Largo's master plan, the crew just try to do their jobs, despite the fact that their assignments rarely make sense, and deadly peril seems to stalk them at every turn.

Set in a future that is both weird and weirdly familiar, Robot Captain is a comic adventure filled with reluctant heroes, strange aliens, lunatic machines, and more than a few twisted surprises.

ISBN 978-1-943219-04-9
51195
9 781943 219049

Available from most online booksellers in hardcover, paperback, and e-book editions. Copies signed by the author can be ordered directly from Space Bear Press at **spacebearpress.com** or from our web store at **https://space-bear-press.square.site/**

www.ingramcontent.com/pod-product-compliance
Lightning Source LLC
Chambersburg PA
CBHW031024190726

48286CB00003BA/999